"I'd never had a friend, and he was my friend; I'd never really, except for a shadowy memory, had a father, and he was my father. I'd never known an adult I could communicate with or trust, and I communicated with him all the time, whether I was actually talking to him or not. And I trusted him . . .

"I knew then that I'd never been close to anyone in my life, not like that. And I wanted to get closer."

ISABELLE HOLLAND was born in Basel, Switzerland, where her father was American Consul. Later, her family lived in Guatemala and then, for twelve years, in England. Ms. Holland received her undergraduate degree from Tulane University. Currently living in New York City, she has written many books including: *Heads You Win, Tails I Lose*; *Hitchhike*; *Alan and the Animal Kingdom*; and *Of Love and Death and Other Journeys*; all are available in Laurel-Leaf editions.

THE MAN WITHOUT A FACE

Isabelle Holland

LAUREL-LEAF BOOKS

Published by
Dell Pubishing Co., Inc.
1 Dag Hammarskjold Plaza
New York, New York 10017

The author gratefully acknowledges permission from the
W. C. C. Publishing Company to include in this book the
poem "High Flight" by Pilot-Officer John Gillespie Magee,
Jr., RCAF. The poem first appeared in the *New York Herald-Tribune* on February 8, 1942.

ISBN: 0-440-96097-5

RL: 5.2

Reprinted by arrangement with J. B. Lippincott Company
Printed in the United States of America

First Laurel-Leaf printing—June 1980
Third Laurel-Leaf printing—October 1981

THE
MAN
WITHOUT
A
FACE

CHAPTER 1

IT WAS THE SUMMER I was fourteen that I came to know the Man Without a Face. Everybody called him that for the obvious reason. Nobody was quite sure how it happened, although the prevailing theory was a car accident plus exploding gasoline. He came in his ancient car to the village near our summer cottage to shop once a week and would stalk into the grocery as though he didn't know that everyone in sight was carefully avoiding looking at him.

The first week we were up there for vacation we almost collided with him as we came out of the grocery. Grudingly he held the door for Mother. He didn't offer to carry any of the heavy bags filled with groceries. The moment we were through, the door slammed behind us.

"You'd think," Mother said, piling bags in the back of the station wagon, "that he'd do something about it. After all. There *is* plastic surgery. That's what it's for. Not just Aunt Tandy's face lift." Aunt Tandy was one of the staples of the summer community. Unkind people said she'd had her face lifted so often that they used a zipper instead of stitches.

"Gruesome," Gloria said. She had come along to the village for the ride so that she could linger over one diet soda at the malt shop in case her current interest, known as Peerless Percy, happened along. Gloria's my sister and one of the main reasons I wanted to get away from home. And now, thanks to her last-minute change of mind, I was in a real mess.

Until this summer Gloria, who is almost seventeen, was going away to boarding school which was why I didn't strain myself about getting into St. Matthew's where, according to family tradition, I was supposed to go at fourteen. With Gloria gone, life would be bearable at home. But then, right before school closed, she finked out and said she didn't want to go to boarding school in the fall after all, after I had more or less deliberately flunked the St. Matthew's entrance exams.

When Mother told me about Gloria's not leaving, I nearly blew my lid. "She's been going to go to that blasted school all her life," I said. "I've been counting on it."

"Well, she's not going now. She says she'd rather stay at home. Frankly, Chuck, I'm delighted. And it wouldn't be such a bad idea if you tried to get on with her. She's older and—let's face it—brighter than you are and can help you a lot with the subjects you seem to be failing."

Tact wasn't one of Mother's strong subjects. But knowing that Gloria's IQ tests always came out at about the genius level (at least that's what Mother told her friends), and mine just average, didn't bug me as much as some other things.

"I don't want to be helped," I said. "Not by Gloria," and split before I got the usual arguments.

That was in the spring. Now it was summer, with still no solution in sight. . . .

Mother and I drove back to the cottage, winding along the shore road. Our community isn't grand enough to sport a yacht club, but there's a white frame house built along one edge of the harbor that acts as a sort of club for the summer people, most of whom have small boats of one kind or another. I was, as usual, thinking about my problem.

"I've got to go to St. Matthew's," I said, after a while.

"Well, you had your chance and you muffed it. You sat for the entrance exam and you flunked it. So how are you going to manage it?"

Yes, how? She had me there, and we both knew it.

As we drove back to the cottage I felt a general depression settle down over me, and took refuge in what I hoped was a dignified silence, glancing in the rear-view mirror every now and then to see if she noticed.

Mother's very pretty—curly brown hair and brown eyes and a triangular face. People say it's like a cameo —whatever that is. Gloria looks liker her and so does Meg, my younger sister. I look like my father, with blond straight sair, kind of greenish eyes and what my last stepfather, The Hairball, used to call a stupid expression. That was after he and Mother decided to divorce. Until then he had tried to be a pal. Mother said once, shortly after they had separated a year ago, and after she had had two martinis and was beginning a third, that I was one of the reasons for the divorce.

"He's marvelous with boys, Chuck. Everyone except you. The kids on the campus liked him. He could always talk to them when they turned off most older people. And I really thought he'd be great for you, since you need a father so badly. But trying to reach you is like trying to break into the First National Bank. Nowhere. You just sit there with that . . . that . . ." She was trying not to say "stupid," because one of the analysts at school had told her she shouldn't use value judgments on me like that. But her control wasn't the greatest at that minute. "That *stupid* look, Charles. And the best man in the world can only take so much of that."

I shrugged. That's one of the things I've learned how to do really well. It saves a lot of trouble and it drives both Mother and Gloria up the wall.

"Don't shrug your shoulders at me," Mother said, her voice rising, as it always does when she has a few drinks.

"Sorry," I said, and got out of the room before she could get a real grip on the conversation.

That exchange had taken place last year just as we came up to the Island for the summer and right after my stepfather informed her that instead of coming up he was going back to his teaching job at Berkeley for summer school, and how about a divorce?

After that Mother drank a little more, got mad at me more often, and took Gloria's side in our fights more often. I've often wondered about all this Oedipus complex stuff you hear about between mother and son. Because it sure hasn't worked with us. Mother doesn't like me. She never has—at least not as far back as I can remember. And I'm not crazy about her. As a matter of fact, I don't much like women of any age. Meg is okay because she's still short and fat and wears braces and hasn't started yet to try to manipulate me. She's eleven. But she's a female, so I am keeping an eye on her, because any day now she may launch on some junior version of the "how could you do this to me?" bit.

Another of Mother's statements, usually after a long, smouldering look is, "You're getting to be just like your father."

"Thanks," I always say, very politely. That also annoys her.

Some women have gardening for a hobby, or good works, or art. Mother's hobby is marrying. So far, and counting the professor who went back to summer school, she has racked up a record of four. There was the first professor, Gloria's father, which probably accounts for Gloria's IQ. I don't know what that divorce was about. Needless to say, I wasn't around. Then there was my father, whom Mother sometimes describes to her friends as "my one real mistake." Once Barry Rumbolt, a widower, who has known her practically all her life and is known generally as Barry Rumble Seat, said bluntly, "Why?"

"Because Eric was so . . . so . . . square and middle-class and true-blue-All-American-Boy-Scout. You know the type. They always turn out to be engineers—or pilots." And she looked across the porch at me.

My repulsive sister Gloria had once gotten hold of a diary I used to keep things I liked and discovered that airplanes were about the most frequent entry. There were a lot of jokes then around the house about "This is your pilot Charles Norstadt. We are now entering a slight turbulence. . . ." Noises of gagging and upchucking would follow. I only got rid of that joke by telling Gloria's latest boyfriend when he called that she had unexpectedly gone back to New York and couldn't go to the weekend dance at the club with him. So of course come that Saturday night, he didn't show. . . . It was very hairy there for a while. But there were no more references to airplanes except the odd one from Mother when she wanted to let me know she found me trying.

"There's nothing wrong with airplane pilots," Barry said. "You like to fly. What if there were no pilots?" That's Barry all over. Old Mr. Reasonable. But what's attractive about being reasonable?

"I like having the garbage picked up, too," Mother said. "But that doesn't mean I want to marry a sanitation worker or have my son devote his life to it as a profession."

I just sat there and swung on the porch glider, grinning, wishing I had brought down a model plane

I had made and put on top of the old-fashioned ward-robe in my room where Big and Little Snoopies couldn't reach without a certain amount of trouble.

"Besides," Mother went on, refilling her glass and Barry's, "this helpmeet in far places bit was not my thing. When Eric got dispatched to Patagonia or Tasmania or outer Slobbovia or wherever it was and wanted me to come along and keep his lunchpail filled, I told him the time had come."

From this you will gather my father was an engineer, a profession that struck Mother as from the boon-docks. She preferred academe or the communicating arts. After she and my father were divorced, she mar-ried Bob, an editor in one of the classier publishing houses in New York, and they spent happy winters having what Barry called "Norman and Irving par-ties." That ended after a raging battle over a review in the *New York Review of Books* of a book that Bob had published. In the middle of the battle Bob dis-covered that Mother hadn't read the book. That did it. He walked out, leaving Mother with Meg as a legacy. Meg has a high IQ too.

After that came another professor. Mother stopped having parties and started protesting. This prof must have been on a dozen committees, because his name kept turning up in those full-page *Times* ads oppos-ing everything and showing up the Establishment. It's the one period in her life when Mother got exercise, carrying pickets of one kind or another. Twice I saw her on television, but one time didn't really count, because there was a counterdemonstration going on across the street, and when she was discovered on camera she had somehow wandered into the opposi-tion. The professor was really annoyed at that.

But nothing annoyed the professor (alias The Hairball) as much as I did, which was fine with me because it was entirely mutual. He would bring his Prophet Ezekiel beard into my room, plunk his big rump down on my bed, and try to buddy up. I don't think he would ever have succeeded, but he scuttled any chance he might have had the second time out. I was sitting at my desk trying to do some homework and he came mooching over.

After irritating me with a lot of small talk, he picked up a small photograph on top of the desk. "Who's the lifeguard type?"

I took it out of his hand and put it in a drawer. "That's my father. And the only time he was a lifeguard was when he was working to get through college."

I'll say this for the prof, he looked sorry on what I could see of his face between the bangs and the beard. "Look, I didn't mean anything by that. It's just a manner of speaking. I'd like us to be friends."

"Sure. But right now I have homework."

He gave a kind of hearty laugh. "Well, maybe I can give you a hand."

"I don't need your help, thanks."

"Your mother says you're not doing so well."

It was true. But it burned me up for him to mention it. I need hardly tell you that Gloria and Meg seemed unable to get anything but A's. I didn't tell him, of course, but I had already made up my mind that the moment I was seventeen I was going to join the Air Force. Once there I could study the things I wanted—even go to college, and then become a pilot. In the meantime, I wasn't killing myself.

"Then," I said, sounding as sarcastic as I could without getting into trouble, "since Mother told you what a dum-dum I am, I'd better get on with memorizing the twice-times. It's pretty difficult."

He mumbled some kind of protest, but I deliberately turned back to my book, which I have found very effective. Being ignored is more than most people can take. Sooner or later they flip their lids and stamp out or just slink to the door. Either way you've won.

The prof was no different, for all his degrees. I looked around a few minutes later and he wasn't there.

He made several tries after that, beginning every other statement with "like" and throwing in "relate to" and "interpersonal relations" as though they were some kind of code words. He even tried getting me hooked on some of his causes—this time the favored words were "relevant" and "involved." Not being the no-brain that he and Mother think I am, I've heard the words before. I even know what they mean and think (privately) they're usually on target. But I wasn't about to discuss anything like that with this hairball—particularly in his role of stepfather.

But he was gone now, anyway, which was altogether a good thing, though being without a husband always brought out Mother's nervous symptoms. For one thing, except when old Barry Rumble Seat was around, it meant she had to go to parties alone. And she didn't like that.

Well, anyway, to get back to the man without a face and how I came to know him. . . .

It began, as I've told you, because of Gloria and her decision to stay at her day school in New York for the next two years. I couldn't put up with that. I already felt I was drowning in women. Funny—when just Mother and Meg and I were home it wasn't so bad. It was even—sometimes—fun. Meg has one reigning interest in life and that is animals, which is another reason that even though she's a female she can't be all bad. Because of Mother's allergies we can't have hairy pets around. So Meg takes out her interest in two aquariums, four turtles, a canary, a budgie, a parrot, and a shelf of books on wildlife. She watches all the animal shows on television and is a charter member of the Flipper Club. When she gets going she can really turn out the information.

And, although it's hard to believe, Mother's a whiz

at telling stories of another kind. Her father had been a scholar of some sort or other and, prompted by Meg or me, she would suddenly break out into some really cool tale about people like Saladin, the Saracen leader during the Crusades, or some Welsh or Bulgarian or Chinese character, that she had picked up by osmosis when she was a child. But she was like that only when Meg and I were alone with her. Gloria and my last two stepfathers put her down if they heard her. As The Hairball once said when he walked in late for dinner and Mother was launched on Robert the Bruce or Cadwallader or Canute or somebody, it retards the development of social consciousness to feed a neurotic need for entirely mythical heroes. And did we know that Robert the Bruce (or Cadwallader or Canute) had scabies and syphilis and body lice? History, he said, sitting down and taking the last of the pot roast, was the chronicle of mass movements, and it was important that Meg and I shouldn't forget it. Mother looked guilt-stricken, and for a second I felt sorry for her. But since she usually made amends for such lapses of social consciousness by pushing me around, my sorrow didn't last long.

Gloria had the same effect on Mother and the general atomosphere as the professor. So I knew, when she dropped her bomb about not going away to school, that I had to get myself out of there. I was due to sit for the entrance exams to St. Matthew's that week, but even though I sat up every night it was too late to catch up the studying I hadn't done. Of course, if I hadn't been as stupid as everyone said I was, I would have studied right along just in case something like this came up. But Gloria had done nothing but talk about the splendors of Fenwick Academy (the finishing school she was supposed to attend) since I could remember. And I had simply not taken into account that with Gloria any on-the-spot heart interest would take priority over everything else, and that New York

was a lot nearer to Princeton and Peerless Percy than
Fenwick, Virginia. Besides which, since I had made
up my mind to split anyway as soon as I had reached
seventeen, I had got it in my head that boarding
school would be a harder place for me to cut loose from
than home, where at least I knew what the setup was.
And so I just didn't bother. And of course, when the
result of the exam came in a letter from the headmaster of the school to Mother, just before we left to
come up here for the summer, I had bombed out.

"And that's that," Mother said, refolding the letter
and not even trying to sound unhappy. She didn't
approve of boarding school for boys anyway. The
Hairball had told her that they turned out a high
percentage of homosexuals, and Mother has a thing
about homos.

So I knew then I was in serious trouble and I had
to do something to get myself to school. So, just before
we left New York, I wrote to the headmaster and
asked him if there were any way—despite my lousy
exam—I could get in.

The answer came the day after we bumped into the
man without a face, whose nickname should, strictly
speaking, have been the man with half a face. One
side of his face was, as Gloria said, gruesome. The
other, if you ever got around to looking at it, which
most people didn't after the initial shock, was okay.
He was also called the Grouch, because no one had
ever known him to say anything that wasn't absolutely
necessary, such as "A loaf of bread and a pound of
coffee, please."

Anyway, in his letter the headmaster said that the
only hope I had was to sit for the exam again at the
end of the summer, at which point—and if I made at
least a B average—my "case would be reviewed."

Of course if St. Matthew's had had any kind of

standing among the prep schools I wouldn't have had a prayer. As Gloria said, when the original result came in, "Who wants a semiliterate WASP?"

But St. Matthew's (where my grandfather and a few great-uncles had gone) had been going into a genteel decline for decades, and though it had a new headmaster, they couldn't be choosy. St Matthew's got what Andover and Exeter and Groton and Choate and the rest of the decent schools wouldn't have. And that was my one hope.

I showed Mother the letter.

"You've never cracked a book during the summer in your life, Chuck. What makes you think you'll do it this time?"

"But if I do, can I go?"

"You're perfectly safe, Mother," Gloria said.

She was sitting at the kitchen table trying on a new set of false eyelashes. "He could no more do the kind of organized studying necessary to drag him from his present first-grade level to even poor old St. Matthew's standard, than he could swim across the harbor. In fact," she picked up her eyelashes off the floor, "since he's more muscle than mind, that's a bad analogy. Do you know what an analogy is, Chuck?" She looked at me with that sweet expression that made me want to kick her.

I knew I was being baited. I also knew I was incapable of coming back with a snappy retort. If snappy retorts ever come to me, it's several hours later or three o'clock in the morning, after I've been lying awake half the night trying to think of them. I ignored her.

"Can I, Ma?"

But Mother had been primed. "Of course. If you think you can."

At the end of the week, I knew Gloria was right: I'd never make it alone. Every night she would ask, usually at dinner, "How's the studying coming, Chuck? Are you on Caesar or Vergil yet?" Or, "I'll be happy to help you with your social studies."

"Fine," I always said, lying through my teeth and digging my own grave, because the more I said it, the less chance I'd ever have of getting any real help.

"That's good," she'd say, looking at me out of her cool brown eyes. "It just shows what you can really do when you try. It's a pity that all these years, what with the tuition bills and everything, you haven't tried before."

I bit. "Why don't you get off my back? If you want to be the head of the local women's lib, try it on your boyfriends, or is that the reason Steve and Larry aren't around this season?"

Now the one thing Gloria doesn't do well (physically, that is) is blush. It comes up like a bad case of measles.

"Spoken with the chauvinism of the stupid male who knows that the only superior thing he has is his musculature." That's her new word, musculature.

"My musculature's great to push your face in with, Glory-old-girl. Let me demonstrate." And I pretended to reach across the table.

Gloria is a physical coward. She panics if you throw a ball at her. "Stop him, Mother," she squeaked.

"If you're going to study, then I suggest you do so," Mother said, stuffing the dishwasher. "After all, it's you who wants to go to boarding school."

I went up to my room and closed the door. Then I stared at the books I had brought up from New York, the ones whose contents would have to be in my head before I had a prayer of getting into St. Matthew's. Maybe all the dreary moralists are right: you have to develop good habits. I had never developed the habit of studying, and now I didn't know where to begin. I went to the kind of school in New York that would rather pass Rosie, the hippopotamus at the Central Park Zoo, than lose the tuition fee. Besides, it was the latest in do-your-own-thing places. No inhibiting structure. No outmoded methods. Lots of Rorschach tests, but no exams.

I have not cried since I was seven years old. I know that doesn't sound possible. But it's true. People who said I was incapable of applying myself to anything didn't know what they were talking about. I had applied myself to not crying—no matter what. Not, you understand, because I'm hung up on being stiff with the upper lip or anything like that. But because it gave Mother some kind of queer hold on me. She loved it. When it *did* happen (before I was seven), I'd find myself pressed against her bosom, half smothered (while Gloria looked on) and for a while after that she'd be very sweet to me, which was nice. But it had a price. She felt then that I was HERS, and until I managed to get some space around me again by being really obnoxious, I could hardly go to the bathroom or make myself a sandwich or go for a walk without her wanting to know where I was going, what I did when I got there, and could she help? Yuch!

Or, if I want to be really truthful, if I had any crying that could not be avoided, I made very sure I was alone and unheard.

The trouble is, our house on the Island was not built for privacy. So I sat on the bed, staring at the books, and trying very hard to think about things that were truly hilarious, like Gloria falling off one of the cliffs around here into a pot of scalding oil. After a while, I turned off the light and got into bed and pushed my face into the pillow.

I must have gone to sleep because the next thing I knew I was awake, the moon was up and there was a low, cushiony growl from the window, followed by a plop on my bed.

"Moxie," I said, and put my arms around him.

The growl turned into a deep, rattling purr. I felt a wet nose against my cheek and smelled bad breath. Poor Moxie. On just about every count you can think of he's socially unacceptable. Moxie's a big yellow tom, with one and a half ears, patches where his fur has been yanked out in his many fights and scars around his face that give him a positively evil expression.

He was a lanky kitten when I found him three years ago. But of course with Mother's allergy, I couldn't keep him or take him to New York. He lives through the winter by hunting and handouts. I have asked some of the native villagers to feed him, offering them money (when I thought they wouldn't be insulted) or doing odd jobs for them during the summer. I guess they do. Feed him, I mean. Or somebody does. Because each summer he's the first thing I look for, and he never misses our arrival. Sometime during the first three nights he comes over the garage roof to my window after it's dark. He knows better than to come to one of the doors during the day. Quite apart from her allergy, Mother hates him. Two years ago she offered to let me keep him officially in my room if I would agree to have him altered. But I knew that this was just part of Mother's wholesale plan for the taming and domesticating of the male species, and I refused.

As a result, Mother takes as a personal slight every ginger kitten around the harbor, and there are more each year.

"Don't let that animal into the house, Charles," she says every now and then for good measure. "He smells and he has bad habits." All true.

"Moxie," I muttered now into his scruffy fur. His purr rattled louder. He stetched his long, battle-scarred body alongside mine. Mother was right about one thing: he stank. He must have been the gamiest thing this side of skunks. But I am the one creature, animal or human, he loves and it's entirely mutual. The only reason I make my own bed in the morning, which otherwise I would consider a concession to female chauvinist imperialism, is to keep Mother from knowing he has been there. With the bed unmade, she would know the minute she hit the door.

Off and on that night I told Moxie about everything in a low voice, while he alternately purred and snored (I think he has a deviated septum or maybe one of his unsuccessful rivals whacked him over the nose). The walls of our house are thin, so I should not have been surprised to see the door open in the early light revealing Meg's tub-shaped form.

"What d'ya want?" I asked surlily.

Meg regarded the two of us. Moxie raised his head. His purring stopped. Without making a sound or moving a muscle, he was, I knew, watching with every hair and sinew. He tolerated Meg. If it had been Gloria or Mother he would have uttered his curious screeching howl and gone through the window in one leap. One of the things I feel I must say about Meg is that even with her thing about animals she isn't jealous, which a lot of animal nuts are. They somehow feel threatened if every creature they meet doesn't leap onto their laps.

She just stood there, her curly hair making her look like a short, fat saint with a halo. "About St. Matthew's," she said.

"What about St. Matthew's?"

"You'll never make it alone."

I opened my mouth to tell her to keep her brilliant insights to herself, but before I could say anything she ploughed on. "It's no use getting on your high horse about it, it's much better to face facts and go on from there."

I mean really, this punk kid, coming over like one of the five psychoanalysts on the staff at school. I opened my mouth again to put her down once and for all when it hit me that that was just what I'd been thinking when I went to bed. All I could say was "So?"

"So, one of the rumors about The Grouch is that he was once a teacher. Maybe he'd coach you."

"You've got to be kidding."

"Why?"

I lay there in the semidark. Why indeed? The rumors about The Grouch, alias The Man Without a Face, alias Justin McLeod were rife.

In our little community everybody knew practically everything about everybody. The one exception was McLeod, who lived off by himself in an old house on the mainland side of the little peninsula that keeps our Island from being a true island. This, of course, made him a fascinating source of gossip: one theory was that he'd been in jail. Another was that he'd been in the CIA and had been firebombed by a double, triple, or quadruple spy. Another was that he was a famous physicist who was living under a pseudonym because an experiment blew up in his face. Then there was the one about the car.

None of us really believed any of them, but with nothing to go on and all summer to speculate the stories got wilder and wilder. One or two of the kids had sneaked onto his property to see what they could nose out, only to be chased off by a huge dog that looked half horse and all homicidal. Everybody got the hint. He didn't want company. So we left him alone.

Now Meg came up with this really tame idea about his having been a teacher.

"Well," Meg said from the door. "You can try it out. All that can happen is for the dog to chew you to pieces."

"Thanks."

I didn't go back to sleep. Moxie relaxed, purred, and even snored a little. But when it grew lighter and the birds started making a racket, his mind obviously turned to breakfast. Also, there was never any telling when the Enemy (Mother or Gloria) would get up and start sending unfriendly waves in his direction. With a final guttural meow and a rub of his head against mine, he gathered his mangy length, sprang to the window and disappeared.

CHAPTER 2

I MULLED OVER MEG'S SUGGESTION the rest of the day, mostly fooling around the pier and the harbor.

"No studying today?" Gloria asked, as I headed towards the porch door after breakfast instead of upstairs.

"I'm taking a day off." What business was it of hers?

"You're that far ahead?" Her expression reminded me of Moxie's when he's bird-watching.

"Leave him alone, Gloria," Mother said from the stove where she was turning bacon over in the skillet.

I waited, standing at the door, for the hooker. It's a running bet with myself. When Mother comes out on my side it usually means something I don't like is on the way. It came.

"Charles, you know I don't like that filthy wild cat in your room and on your bed at night. He smells up the whole house."

How did she know?

Raging, I looked at Meg. But without even looking up from spooning her heaping bowl of cereal she was shaking her head. And I knew that bratty as she sometimes is, Meg wouldn't nark on me.

But there sat Gloria, picking at her scrambled egg like she was the heroine of that moronic story about a princess and a pea that Mother used to read to us when we were both small. I think Gloria got her permanent self-image from that female.

"Thanks," I said, looking right at her.

"Does it occur to you," she said languidly, "that your feline friend is crawling with parasites? You can practically see them keeping house in his fur."

Since Moxie's tail balloons out and his back arches every time he sees Gloria, I don't think it's his parasites that bug her (if you'll excuse the pun).

"Yes, but he has such good taste in people," I said, rather pleased with myself for once. "Besides, I thought you were big on wildlife and ecology—or was that just until Steve decided he could live without you?"

Gloria's face went psychedelic pink. "You rat. You wait. Mother—"

But I was out the porch door and down the steps. That kind of conversation had been going on almost as far back as I could remember and I wanted out.

There weren't too many kids of my age around this summer. Some from last year had gone off to camp or another summer place, and my best friend, Joey Rodman, who also goes to my school in New York, was still in Europe with his parents where they were force-feeding him culture in the hope of boosting his IQ. That's what drew us together: IQ. And, if anything, his case is even worse than mine, because, as he says, if you're Jewish with a ho-hum IQ, man, you're in real trouble. The family looks on it as a disgrace second only to converting to Christianity. But Joey wasn't here now when I needed him, so after exchanging a few insults with a couple of kids bailing out a dinghy, I walked along the harbor skipping stones and thinking about what Meg said.

After several dreary hours relieved only by four

hot dogs, a hamburger and an occasional ice cream cone, bought whenever I circled back to the village, I came to see that it was all summed up in the question: What's the alternative?

And the alternative was living for the next three or four years in a five-room apartment in New York, with my snotty older sister putting me down every time she sees me, having to walk through a forest of wet stockings and underwear every time I want to take a shower and trying to find my toothbrush in a jungle of false eyelashes, hair pieces, makeup glop, and I don't know what all. And if I complained Mother would take Gloria's side. There's no dignity in living crashed in a small pad with a bunch of women. So, wondering how it felt to be chomped on by a man-hating dog, I went off to look for Justin McLeod.

It was a fairly long walk and uphill most of the way. Between thoughts of The Grouch and his dog the butterflies in my stomach were threatening to become bats, so to keep my mind occupied I tried to remember everything I had ever heard about Justin McLeod. It wasn't difficult. The answer was all but zilch. Totted up, the items amounted to:

1. He had come to live in the house on the cliff about twelve years ago. Occasionally he closed the house and went away. But not often.

2. He lived there alone with his carnivorous dog, which meant that nobody who had dredged up some excuse or other to call on him and poke around had gotten much beyond the gate. There was a sort of P.S. to this, that the dog had been known to devour small children, but I dismissed that as unlikely. The whole thought about the dog was depressing me, so I went on to

3. Despite all the really interesting theories as to how he got his mutilation and his past in general, the only reliable evidence of professional activity was that he received letters and parcels from some publishing

house in New York. Some of the letters had windows in them and looked as though they might be checks. (I'm not sure how this was known. The postmistress is a glacial female who seems to view her job as a Vocation. She looks as though she wished hot pincers could be applied to her fingernails by Communist agents so she could heroically refuse to tattle about who gets what mail in the village. Despite this, somebody had talked, and there was a fairly well accepted idea that, whatever else might have been, McLeod was a writer.)

4. The trouble with item 3 is that no one had ever seen his name on a book. This gave rise to the hypothesis (if you'll excuse one of Gloria's show-off words) that

5. He writes pornography under a pseudonym.

The moment this theory took hold, everybody—that is, all the young people—descended on our one bookstore and, when that proved to be a bust, on the store in the nearest town on the mainland, to buy up all the porno and go through it for what the sleuth novels call internal evidence. But all they found was the usual dreary run of reprint paperbacks. Not one real hard-core porno among them. But then as Joey pointed out (his father's in publishing), you could hardly expect any, this being a very backward and uptight part of the country.

All these cogitations got me nowhere except, physically, where I was going.

McLeod's house is on top of a cliff, several miles north of the harbor, and you have to go around the long way to get to his gate, the only opening in a stone wall built by some people-hating New Englander of the past. On the other side of the gate you can see bunches of pines and a path winding through them. The house is hidden from the road and the whole thing is pretty bleak. There was no sign saying

"Beware of the Dog." Still, I loitered there for a few minutes, and by doing so saved myself (I thought) a lot of trouble. Because I heard the sound of an engine and round the path came McLeod's venerable but still rather handsome foreign car. Stopping, he got out, and I saw he was going to open the gate. I could have kicked myself then for failing to make a good impression by springing to attention and doing it for him. But I didn't think fast enough (as usual). He's a big man and he covered the few feet to the gate before the idea clicked. He stared at me over the gate as he unlatched it, and it was like a cold wind coming at me. "What do you want?" were the words he said. His *voice* said *Keep away from me*.

Everything I had been planning to say, a kind of savvy introduction to my problem, went out of my head. For one thing, there was his face, closer than I had seen it before. And it was pretty unnerving. Glazed raw beef all over most of one side and flowing across his nose to the other. I just stared, then pulled my gaze off his face as though my eyes were suction cups, looked down, sideways, above, anywhere but at him, shuffled my feet like a rube, and stammered, "I —I h-heard you were a t-teacher—once."

Silence. "So?"

Gazing at the nearest pine I mumbled, "I was wondering if you could c-coach me. I n-need to pass an entrance exam."

"No. Certainly not."

And he got back in the car and drove through the gate.

After he had gone I realized how I had really loused it up. To tell you the truth, I could have cried. I leaned with my elbows on the stone wall for a while. I couldn't go back to the house. I just couldn't. After a while I sat down with my back against the wall. Why did I always do things the wrong way? Why did nothing ever come out right?

I knew it was getting colder and darker. I was facing east and the sky was turning charcoal gray. The wind whistled and whispered through the pines. I had just a loose sweat shirt on and jeans, and I was beginning to realize the grass wasn't all that dry. But I couldn't make myself move. It would be dinner before too long. I hadn't been back to the house all day and if I didn't show at dinnertime I'd have to go through everything I hated most:

"How could you be so inconsiderate?"

"How can you be so irresponsible?"

Or, the real joker in the pack, "The truth is, Chuck, you just don't care about anybody but yourself—you don't love me." Followed by Mother in tears. Followed by me wishing I were dead.

It finally turned dark, but I still couldn't move. I pulled my knees up and rested my head on them. Poor old third-rate St. Matthew's seemed like a vanished golden dream. And then, inside of me, I just quit. Turned everything off. Nothing mattered. Periodically this happens to me. Sooner or later I snap out of it, or something snaps me back, but for a while I'm not there, if you know what I mean, though I guess if it hasn't happened to you you don't. But it is what has made all five school analysts rush around trying to be helpful from time to time. When I finally come out of it and there they are, still making noises and jumping up and down, I usually think it's pretty funny. But until I do, it's like everything is going on in another galaxy and anyway, what's the point?

I raised my head to see two headlights focused on the gate. I hadn't even heard the engine, but McLeod and his car were back. I watched while he pulled the gate-bars back, but instead of getting into the car he came towards me.

"Why haven't you gone home?" he asked in that knifey voice.

What could I say? My mind was absolutely blank. So I said nothing and sat there like a dummy.

"Get up!"

I got up, but I had been sitting so long I half stumbled. Wherever my jeans had touched the grass they were wet. The night wind was cold, as it always is up around here. I was cold inside and out and I knew I had to get home and into a hot bath if I didn't want to get one of the chills this area is famous for.

"Where do you live?"

"T-the other s-side of the h-h-harbor." It wasn't a stammer this time. My teeth were chattering.

"Do you know you've been here for nearly four hours? What have you been doing?"

When I didn't answer he took my arm in a punishing grip and pushed me towards the car. "Get in."

Instead of turning around and taking me back to the Island, he drove through the gate and up the path, not stopping to close it again.

Sure enough, the Hound of the Baskervilles came out to greet us baying as though he could hardly wait for his dinner: me.

"All right, Mickey. Shut up!"

Mickey. Like calling a Bengal tiger Cuddles.

"Get out," McLeod said, leaning across me and pushing my door open.

When there is absolutely no alternative, I can be quite brave, and with McLeod blocking one exit and Sudden Death shoving his great jaw through my window, what choice did I have?

"Go on," McLeod said. "He won't hurt you. Not as long as you're with me."

I got out. Mickey reared. His doomsday voice bayed again. I closed my eyes.

"Sit!" McLeod said.

I opened my eyes. Mickey was sitting on his

haunches, his head on a level with my shoulders, his tongue hanging out like a chopping block.

"Are you coming?" McLeod said, standing at the open front door.

A long time afterwards Mother or someone asked me what the house was like inside. No one had ever been there—at least not within memory. All anyone knew was that it had belonged in one family for quite some time. But no one living now in the village had ever been up there. I don't know what they expected. Dracula's lair? Cobwebs from the ceiling?

Anyway, I wasn't in much of a state to notice anything that night.

"Go straight ahead through that door at the end of the hall," he said, when I stumbled over the threshold. "The light's on. I'll be there in a minute."

The door led into a smaller hall and then into a kitchen. It was a big room with a stone floor and low ceiling. An old-fashioned lamp, giving out a yellow light, hung from a rafter. There was a sink along one side beneath a window, a big table in the middle, and a chair. Along the other side was what Mother would call an old-fashioned iron range and open grate, and from it came a delicious heat. I backed up to it and was all but sliding my buttocks across the warm top when the door burst open and the dog loped in. Seeing me, he stopped. A bass growl started in the huge throat. I stood rigid. McLeod followed, holding a glass with some golden liquid. "Quiet," he said to Mickey. To me he said, "Drink this," and handed the glass to me.

I did, and it burned all the way down.

"Now go through that door and up the stairs and into the bathroom at the top of the staircase. I've drawn some hot water. Get in and stay in long enough to get warm. Then get out, dry off and put on the clothes you find there. They'll be big but they'll have to do. Then come back down again. Now move!"

I didn't argue, whether I had been softened up by the drink or because I was too chilled or because of something in his voice.

I was down again in about twenty minutes, warm, dry, and rather drowsy. The dark blue sweater I had on was like a tent. The trousers were folded halfway up to the knee and I had to use the belt he'd left out, but he must be leaner than I thought because they weren't that loose. I was carrying my own sodden garments.

He was standing staring out the window above the sink to the sea beyond and below when I came back in, his profile to me. In the half light from the lantern and from that side his disfigurement wasn't that visible. Whatever had happened to him had not touched the bones of his face, which were good, with the nose slightly aquiline, the forehead high and the jaw firm. Then he turned and became Quasimodo again. It wasn't just the awful red. The scars were here and there gathered or pitted like a relief map.

"All right?" he said.

I nodded. "Yes, thanks."

"There's some tea on the table. Drink it."

I never much cared for being ordered around, but somehow I didn't protest. The tea was hot, sweet, strong and had milk in it. On the whole it tasted good and cleared my head some. I remembered what I was here for.

"You can leave the clothes at the grocery store," he said. "I'll pick them up when I next shop. Now I'll drive you home."

"Look, about coaching," I started desperately.

"I said no." He turned the lamp down again and started towards the door. What I had half taken to be a large rug in front of the fireplace got up and became Mickey. There was nothing to do. I followed them through the house and out the front door. Mickey was left sitting on the front step as McLeod and I drove down the road to the gate.

We were going along the high cliff road, the sea far below, the lights of the village off to one side and curving around the little harbor, when I said something stupid, even for me. "I'll pay you," I said. "There's money Dad left me and I've saved quite a lot. You can have all of it. It's more than three thousand dollars."

"I don't want your money." He said it in a perfectly ordinary voice but I felt ashamed.

"Did I—did I say something wrong?"

"I don't know. Did you? Did you intend to?"

"No. Truly. It's just—" My voice trailed off. Explaining Mother—let alone Gloria, the feeling that the corner I was in was getting smaller and smaller, Gloria at home all next winter, and the next, and the next—how could I explain that?

This is where girls cry, I suppose, and for a minute, only a minute, I wished I could, if it would wash away that tight, burning feeling inside me that was getting tighter and more burning. But I couldn't. I rolled down the window to let the air cool my face and stared at the dark wall of trees rushing by.

After a minute McLeod said, "What's the exam for?"

"St. Matthew's."

"Why is it so important for you to go there?"

When I had gone up to his house I had the whole thing laid out, what I would say, and so on. It would have moved Grant's Tomb. Now, thanks to the brandy or whiskey he gave me, everything was hopelessly confused. I tried to recapture the manly, straightforward sentences I had put together. Nothing came.

"Well?" He sounded exasperated.

I knew I had to say something even though I didn't

think he had the slightest intention of changing his mind. He'd undoubtedly think it was a big joke, the jerk. But what choice did I have?

I drew a long breath. "Because I'm sick of living at home with three women, my mother and two sisters, particularly since they're both brighter than me and make nothing but A's—my sisters, I mean. I thought Gloria, my older sister, the one who— Well, anyway, she was going away to boarding school. Now she's not. She's going to be home all winter and the year after that and the year after that. Messing me up. Putting me down. Making fun of everything I do. When I'm seventeen I'm going to join the Air Force. But that's three years away and I can't stand it."

"I see," he said. "What's your name?"

"Charles Norstadt."

He put the car in gear and we drove down onto the peninsula and then turned right into the road that curled around the harbor and went past our house on the other side.

"All right. I'll coach you. But you'll have to do it my way, and that means the hard way. You must have sat for the exam already. St. Matthew's doesn't give the second exam unless it's necessary. I take it you failed?"

"Yes," I whispered, terrified he would change his mind.

"Did you study for it?"

"No."

"If you wanted to get in so much, why not?"

I explained again about Gloria's change of plan.

"That wasn't very farsighted, was it?"

"No." Scared as I was that he would back out, I knew I might as well get one thing cleared up from the beginning. "I'm not terribly bright. Not like my sisters, anyway."

"Who told you that?"

"Practically everybody—besides, they have tests at school."

"What school did you go to?"

I told him. He didn't say anything.

Then, "Where, by the way, do you live?"

"The first house on the land side past the dinghy pier."

He stopped a few yards short of the house. "All right. Be at my house tomorrow morning at eight. I'll coach you three hours every morning five days a week, and I'll give you enough work to take you another three hours. That's six hours a day during what should be your vacation. It will be tough. But if I ever find you haven't done the work I've assigned you, you won't come back. Are you sure it's worth it?"

So with my usual luck I had found myself another Hitler.

Repressing a desire to say *Sieg heil* with a snappy arm salute like in the movies, I said, "Yes. Sir."

I could see right away we were going to have a lovely summer, he and I. But he didn't need me. I needed him. And we both knew it. And to add to everything else, I would have to look at him three hours a day five days a week. I know it sounds pretty awful to say that, like not wanting to be seen with a cripple. But I can't help it. The only thing it's less awful than is being around Gloria for the next three years.

"Where've you been?" Mother asked as I walked through the back door into the kitchen. "Do you know what hour it is?"

"Nine," I said, knowing it was after ten, and trying to get across the room as fast as possible.

"It's ten thirty. And don't walk out of the room while I'm talking to you. Have you had dinner?"

"Yes," I lied, still moving towards the door to the back staircase.

"Where?"

I was thinking furiously, because until that moment it hadn't occurred to me that I wasn't going to tell her about McLeod's coaching me. But it was as though the decision were already made and all I had to do was to find some acceptable explanation for being out so late and arriving home in strange clothes. My own I had strung on the back line as I passed on the way in.

"And whose clothes are those?" Gloria asked, as though she had been cued by what was going on in my head.

"Pete Lansing's. I fell off the dock and Barney lent me these." Barney was Pete's younger brother. Pete was in Vietnam and therefore unavailable for questioning. And Barney would play dumb. Besides, he was due to go off to camp almost any day.

"I wish you'd be more careful," Mother said. "You might hit your head on a rock and really hurt yourself. This isn't Florida or Long Island with nothing but sand at the bottom."

"First you have to have something in your head to hurt," Gloria drawled, like some old Bette Davis heroine. She eyed McLeod's pants. "I didn't know Pete was that tall," she said. "And you could get two of him in that sweater."

"Maybe just being away from you was enough to get his vitamins working," Meg said, to my astonishment. She was sitting at the table reading, drinking a malted, and working her way through a box of chocolate chip cookies. It's true that Pete Lansing had once seemed to have the hots for Gloria, along with all the other older boys. But none of them ever stayed that way for long. Which was one reason why our Gloria was so sour. Or maybe it was the other way around.

"You keep on stuffing yourself," Gloria said to

Meg, "and there won't be any guys around you at all."

.Meg took another cookie. But I could see her cheeks get red. One good turn deserves another. "She may not get as many as you," I said pointedly, "but seven gets you eight that anybody who likes her will go on liking her. Besides, you can lose fat, but there's not much you can do about a naturally repulsive personality."

Gloria doesn't get red when she gets mad, the way Meg does. She gets white, and for a minute there she looked like skim milk. She got up. "Let's see the label in those pants," she said, and snapped out a hand toward me.

Now that was pretty cute of her. Pete was a snob about jeans, which he called Levi's. Only the genuine cowpoke's would do. His came from Jackson, Wyoming, where he had worked on a ranch part of every summer before he went into the army. I don't know where McLeod got the ones I was wearing, but the chances of their coming from Jackson, Wyoming, were about zero.

There happened to be a ruler on the table; why, I don't know. But there it was like the serpent in the Garden of Eden and of course I picked it up and whacked her hand away. I guess I hit harder than I really intended. . . .

The only thing I can say about what followed is that it took everybody's mind off where I had been and what I'd been doing.

Mother's lecture went on for what felt like half an hour while she bathed Gloria's hand and mopped up the blood from the cut across her palm. The thin steel plate along the edge of the ruler had sliced the inside of her hand and it was no use my saying that it wasn't deliberate. With Gloria sobbing as though she'd been attacked with a switchblade and Mother going on and on about my dangerous temper and what it had done to my father, who was listening?

"You'll apologize to Gloria, do you hear me?" Mother said, as I tried again to split by the back staircase. "If you don't we'll come up and stay in your room until you do."

What I would have given to say "So stay!" But Mother had learned early that that was the one threat that worked. All the rest of the house—or the apartment in New York—was theirs. My room was mine and I'd pay the price, usually an apology, to keep it that way. I turned and came down the stairs.

"I'm sorry," I said, lying in my teeth and with my fingers crossed behind my back. *I hope you get tetanus and die*, was what I thought to myself. And then a kind of superstitious horror took hold of me. *I didn't mean that, God,* I thought quickly. *Undo it, please.* I didn't want that on my conscience.

In the middle of what The Hairball used to call this *Sturm und Drang,* Old Barry Rumble Seat pushed open the screen door and came in.

"Hiya," he said, as though it were midafternoon and everybody was sitting around having sweetness and light.

"Hello," Meg said.

"Hi, Sweetheart."

Meg digs Barry. Why, I can't think, unless it's what's called a community of suffering. They're both overweight. She gave him her best grin which even with braces and cookie crumbs packs a lot of voltage.

He grinned back. "What's going on?"

What with the Band-Aids all over the table and the disinfectant making the kitchen smell like a hospital and Gloria sitting there with her blotched tears acting like a rape case, I can see why he'd ask. But it was the lead-in that Gloria the Wronged must have been praying for. As I eased out she was sounding her favorite theme. "Something simply has to be done about Chuck's paranoid attacks. With his background and his father being the way he was. . . ."

I got into my room, just barely managing not to slam the door. Gloria, the fink, knows where to shove in the needle, which is one reason why she is so universally beloved. . . .

I kicked the wastebasket and stood there, watching the paper and candy wrappers and peanut shells ricochet off the walls all over the rag rug, thinking how stinking lousy everything was. Six hours' work a day, Himmler McLeod, and if everything worked, a crummy boarding school in the fall where they probably goose-stepped you off to chapel six times a day.

"But you got what you wanted," said the Judas voice inside me that always speaks up when I am about to enjoy my own misery.

During the course of the night I contemplated my readymade decision not to tell Mother or Gloria about McLeod coaching me, although I might tell Meg since it had been her idea. But nobody else, because in a summer community like ours it would get back in less than twenty-four hours. I'm not sure why I felt so strongly about this, beyond the usual reason that if Gloria ever discovered that something was important to me, she'd mess it up if she could.

You'd think, considering the way we feel about each other, that she'd be *happy* to have me in boarding school when she's home. But it isn't so. The only thing I can figure is that it's some kind of power thing with her. Once, long ago, when Gloria was up to her usual bag of tricks, I asked Mother, "Why does she act like that to me? I mean—what did I ever do to her?"

Mother was ironing at the time and I think we were up here on the Island. I do remember she was wearing shorts and a long pink shirt abandoned by one of her husbands. With her dark hair down she looked, I swear, younger than Gloria—more like Meg after a successful diet. Anyway, she ironed for a minute, then said. "You got born, Charles, that's what you did to her."

"But that's not my fault."

"No. But when she was three, which is when you were born, she didn't know that. All she knew was that somebody had arrived to take not only my attention away from her, but also her brand-new stepfather's whom she was already flirting with."

"But she hated my father. She's always telling me what a jerk he was—the way you do."

That was one of those minutes when I had the curious feeling that something that might have made me understand the whole business between Mother and me almost happened but didn't quite. For a minute she looked terribly unhappy—sort of stricken. When she looks like that a queer desire to protect her comes over me and I have to hold onto myself and remember that if I give in the gates will clang to and lock behind me. So I clenched my teeth and said nothing.

"Charles—I never meant. . . . I didn't want. . . ."

I wanted to tell her everything was all right and I didn't mean it. (Mean what? I wasn't sure, but it didn't matter.) I wanted to kiss her cheek and tell her I'd take care of everything. Yes, I did. It's incredible, but I did. I remember it very well—and then the door opened and Gloria walked in. Mother's face closed up. She turned her back to pick up something else to iron and when she turned around again she just said, "We didn't always feel like that about him."

We, I thought. All of a sudden she and Gloria were a team again. They were on one side and Dad and I were on the other and never the twain would meet and all that jazz. Only it's a little lopsided, be-

cause I can barely remember my father. I remember
a big man with blond hair like mine and a smile,
and his putting me on his shoulders that felt about
a mile high. The sea was behind him. I remember
the feeling more than the way it looked. And the
feeling was being happy. Like everything was relating
to everything else and making sense.

Anyway, I knew that apart from my freaked-out
sister, it would not be a good idea for me to broadcast
the fact that I was going to be hobnobbing with The
Man Without a Face. People were leery of him and
Mother is conventional. She doesn't like anyone going around doing oddball things. And McLeod was
definitely an oddball.

My absence during the day needn't cause any flutter
because I was nearly always up and out before the
rest of the family and down with the kids in the
harbor. More often than not I wouldn't touch base
again till dinnertime. So there'd be no problem there.
It all looked very neat. Now all I had to do was to
get the books I had brought to the Island up to Mc-
Leod's house, and there was a hefty load of them.

CHAPTER 3

I ARRIVED, sweating, at McLeod's gate at seven thirty the next morning, lugging the books in two shopping bags I had stolen from the kitchen, after occasional rests on the way.

After puffing a bit I pushed the gate open and started up the path. Sure enough, there was a familiar, bone-crunching growl, and my great friend Mickey bounded around the bend. I stood stock still.

"Good Mickey," I said, pinning my hope to flattery.

The huge beast came straight at me. I closed my eyes. There was silence. I knew I was still alive because I could feel my heart beating. Very slowly, I opened my eyes. Mickey was sitting two feet from me, tongue out, ears forward, head on one side. Behind him about twenty feet was McLeod. On top of a horse.

"You're early."

"Yes."

"What are the bags for?"

"Books from school."

"You needn't have brought them. I have others." I thought, Thanks a lot for telling me. McLeod's horse was sure nervous. He kept backing and sidling and tossing his head, which was queer, because his rein wasn't tight. I looked to see if McLeod had on some kind of a spur, which would be just like him, but he didn't. The horse was really beautiful, a goldeny bay. Next to airplanes I like horses.

"Why's he so nervous? Your horse?"

"Because you're standing there. He doesn't like strangers. Go on up to the house."

You could see just how psychotic the man was, I thought, as I lugged the books up that practically ninety-degree incline. Well—at least forty-five degree. I have ridden on and off most of my life whenever I could get a chance, and it's been my observation that it's the rider that makes a horse nervous, not some inoffensive bystander—particularly when he's already being threatened by man's best friend, Mickey.

A few minutes later I came through the last clump of trees and now, in daylight, got the whole effect of the headland, with the house on it, and it was really something. At least, the view was. The house faced straight into the Atlantic, which this morning, under the early sun, was kind of a gauzy purple, a little blurred at the horizon. From where I was standing the top of the cliff seemed to jut halfway to the sky. Nothing below—the rocks, the peninsula, the harbor, and the village, which I knew were off to the right— was visible. Between me and the house was a wide stretch of grass, and dotted here and there were some trees, gnarled and bent backward.

The house was old, you could tell by the roof and the windows and the walk on top of it. And there was something about the house, maybe because it needed a coat of paint, that made me think about that widow's walk and how some woman had walked around it for hours and days and maybe years, watching and hoping for a ship that never made it home. It was that kind of a house.

I was standing there gawking (and resting for the

umpteenth time) when I heard the sound of hooves back and to the left. Turning, I saw McLeod leap the bay over a barred gate between two trees at the end of what looked like a path going down through the trees in another direction. Then he cantered back of me to a small barn attached to the other side of the house. Dismounting, he took the horse in.

When he came out and towards the front door I was waiting.

"It's open," he said curtly.

I opened the door and walked into the hall that I vaguely remembered from the night before. In the daylight it looked smaller. There were wide oaken floor planks, the staircase. No carpet, just a chest along one wall.

"To your left," McLeod said, coming up behind me.

We went into a big room. The outside of the house might be crummy, but the inside was really together. That is, if you like books. There were two walls of them. There was also a big desk near the windows that looked over to the cliff, a table, and two big chairs.

"Put the books there on the table," McLeod said. He had on dark pants of some kind stuffed into rough-looking boots and a gray sweater. It was hard to tell what age he was. He was lean and athletic-looking, but his hair had as much gray scattered throughout as it did black and the half of his face that wasn't raw steak was lined. Maybe forty, maybe fifty.

I hauled the bags over and emptied out the books. McLeod turned them over. "All right," he said, after a while. He went over to the desk and opened a drawer. "Here's some paper. Write me three hundred words on any subject you choose."

Straight off he hit a nerve. I don't like to write—at least not for school. "But that's not part of—" I waved my hand towards the books, "of what I have to know."

"I thought you agreed to do it my way."

"Yes, but—"

"But what?"

"I have to bone up on social science, math, Latin, and English."

"This is English composition, or hadn't it occurred to you?" Pause. "Haven't you ever written any compositions?"

"Not for a while—and besides, they're not going to ask me to do one for the exam."

"How do you know?"

"They didn't last time."

"All right, Charles. Pick up your books. I'll drive you as far as the Peninsula Bridge."

We had a little silence while I hated him. Mickey, in front of the unlit fireplace, found a flea and went to work on it. I thought about the Air Force and whether if I stuffed vitamins and exercised all summer I could con them into believing I was seventeen. And I knew the answer to that. No.

"We do it my way or not at all," McLeod said, in case I had missed the point, which I hadn't.

"Don't I have any say at all?" I knew the answer to that, too. Who the freaking blazes did he think he was? A teacher, of course, the kind I had forgotten about. Learn my way or else.

"All right," I said, staring down at the table.

"Look at me!"

Stubbornly, I didn't.

"I said look at me."

I can't say his voice was any louder, but despite my determination not to, I snapped my head up sharp and fast.

"Now listen to me, Charles. I'll say this once and that's all. I agreed to coach you out of a moment of —pity—that I now regret. But I keep my word. And if you stay you're going to keep yours. I'm not going to explain my teaching. I'm not interested in your

good opinion. I don't care whether you like me or
hate me. But you're going to pass that exam, and if
at any moment I think you're not, because you're not
doing what I tell you, then we stop. Is that clear? Do
you accept it? Because if you don't—entirely—you
can leave now."

The "pity" was deliberate; even in the midst of the
rage I felt, I knew that. And it made everything clear
to me—the needling, the bullying: he wanted out. But
he didn't have the guts to tell me he'd changed his
mind. People like him don't ever admit to changing
their minds. They make you do it for them. I realized that in one way he'd really won the brass ring—
he'd made Gloria look almost good. But—for the moment—she'd stopped being that important. Then, inside, I started turning it all off because it was all so
wormy. I could feel myself doing it. Things began
not to hurt so much. I was backing, at least in my
mind I was, and he was watching me. There was a
line going from the side of his nose on the unscarred
side down to his mouth. It made him look mean as
a snake, I decided. And his eyes, pinched deep into
the burned flesh, were so pale it was like looking
through windows into nothing. I heard my voice, almost as though it were coming from a distance.

"I'm staying."

"Why?"

Because I hate your guts, was the reason. "I want
to pass the exam."

"Are you sure?"

"Yes. I'm sure." It was queer how calm I suddenly
felt.

He nodded towards the sheets of lined paper. "All
right. Three hundred words."

I did his lousy three hundred words, sitting there
at the table while he sat in one of the comfortable
leather chairs and went again through the books I
had brought, and Mickey lay in front of the empty

fireplace, snorting and twitching as he dreamed of chasing rabbits, or more probably people. My only pain was in getting the thousand words of the original essay by Jake Rodman, Joey's older brother, down to three hundred.

Jake had won a prize with it at his school, which was luckily not Joey's and mine, and his proud mother had saved it. I had already used it three times on three different teachers—with a different title each time—and the first time I was told that at last I was showing not only creative talent but a maturing social consciousness. The original title was *Why The System Must Be Changed*. When Jake wrote it, it was published in his school paper and a team of upperclassmen debated it before the assembled school, faculty and parents. It was a really big deal. His parents were so pleased they gave him a trip to Europe and the school persuaded him to put in an application to Harvard, which accepted him. How could I do any better? Joey had offered it to me when I was about to cut my throat over a paper I couldn't hack, saying no one would know. So I changed a few words here and there, just for safety's sake, and turned it in.

Boy! Did I ever get the blue ribbon treatment there for a bit. Even our junior SDS chapter looked impressed. It was really exhilarating. So, when I had to do another paper a year later in English, I doctored a few more words, changed the title once more, put in a large quote that Joey found in the current *Ramparts* mag, and turned it in again. It, too, got an A— the second one in my life. The English teacher was not turned on to the school scene as much as the social science guy since, as he explained, he was undergoing therapy and his shrink felt that his libido had to be chiefly directed towards his psychodrama class that met every night. This was after he had gone to sleep in class while we read aloud Ginsberg's poem "Howl," and discussed its relevance to the current revolution. One or two of the reactionary kids suggested he might be strung out on pot, but the responsible leaders shouted them down and told them any more such counterrevolutionary garbage and they wouldn't get out of the school yard with all their parts. . . . Anyway, the teacher's libido being otherwise occupied, he didn't make a big thing out of the essay, I mean read it aloud or anything, which was just as well, since quite a few of the kids in class would have recognized it in a minute. He just gave me an A. So, heartened by all this success and feeling that there was no point in abandoning what was so obviously a good thing, I tried it once more on the new current events teacher. . . .

Well, after all the dust settled, and Mother had been summoned to the principal's office and I went the round of the school analysts again, I realized I had overdone it, and there was plainly some truth in the hoary old cliché *Moderation in everything.* . . .

However, Quasimodo-Ivan-the-Terrible McLeod hadn't been exposed to it, and by this time I pretty well knew it by heart. So, occasionally stopping to frown into the fireplace or chew my ball-point pen for effect, just in case he might be looking, I hotted the old stew and served it up.

It was a mistake, and I saw instantly that I should have known it would be. He flipped through it like lightning.

"So," he said when he had read it, "You are a ponderer on social issues. Who would have thought it?"

It seemed safest not to say anything.

"It's a pity that your grasp of the major contemporary problems is not equaled by your mastery of spelling and grammar."

Well I could answer that one. "Grammar is a racist device for repressing the language of the people."

"Indeed? Well, I am afraid that you're either going to have to abandon your revolutionary principles regarding grammar and spelling, or give up your idea of getting into St. Matthew's. Which is it going to be? They're extremely reactionary about things like grammar and spelling."

"I thought St. Matthew's was supposed to be third-rate—practically anybody could get in."

"Apparently you couldn't."

"Well, you know what I mean."

"You mean a school where you can get away with the rubbish you've been used to turning in at your current establishment—like this, for instance." And he threw the sheets of paper onto the table.

Gingerly I felt my way. "You mean you think it's wrong?"

"Whether it's right or wrong is not the point. You didn't write it."

Right on. But how did he know? None of the others I had offered it to had, not even the last one, until in his initial enthusiasm he had started to read it aloud to the class and got instant feedback.

"Did you?" The strange, light gray eyes bored into me over puffy cliffs of red flesh.

"No."

"Who did?"

"Jake Rodman. He's the older brother of my best friend, Joey. He's now at Harvard." I don't know why I added that, maybe to show him that I copied only the eighteen-karat best.

He surprised me by giving a short laugh, only there was more bite than ha-ha in it. "If you ever give me anything phony again, the old rules as stated apply. Out. Remember, it's your choice. Do you want to learn or not? You came to me. Not I to you. Just who's doing whom a favor?" After another of our silences he said, "Have you ever written anything entirely of your own?"

Back to the sore nerve. "Yes."

"What was it about?"

I saw I couldn't dodge the issue so I said grudg-ingly, "It was about an airplane, like it was a per-son; how it got started and how it felt when it first took off."

"Well? What happened? What did you get on it?"

"The teacher said it was ungradable."

"Why?"

It was an occasion I don't really care to remember. The new social science teacher had pulled the same trick as McLeod—write something on any subject you want. So I did this thing on the plane. How was I to know that he went rabid over any invention since the wheel, that he was a one-man antitechnocracy lobby?

Well, by the time he got through with my paper everybody knew. You would have thought it was Bob Hope up there, as he read aloud with expressions and gestures and a kind of between-sentences run-ning commentary. He had them rolling between the desks. It was one of the great comic turns of the school year. Except I didn't find it so funny. When he finished and took out his handkerchief and wiped his eyes and got serious he gave the class a pep talk on ecology and nature and living in harmony with the earth and what America and technocracy had done to ruin the planet. Then he tore the paper up and threw it into the wastebasket and went on to the next. . . .

Even The Hairball, who was then married to Moth-er, said the teacher had gone a bit far, after he and the police had tracked me down on the New Jersey Turnpike where I was trying to hitch a ride to Colo-rado. (The Air Force Academy is in Colorado, and while I knew I didn't have a chance of getting in—certainly not at my age and without at least a high school certificate—I thought I could nose around long enough and be near enough to learn the best approach. But I only got as far as the first gas station past the tunnel!)

McLeod was staring at me. I couldn't think of anything to say. I mean, absolutely nothing occurred to me.

"Well, why did he say it was ungradable?"

I took a careful breath. "He hates planes. You know—ecology, antitechnocracy, all that jazz. Can I go now?" I didn't know whether or not the three hours were up, but I wanted to get out.

"Not for another hour. We'll have to go over what you have to cover by the end of the summer and I'll give you your assignment for tomorrow."

He finally sprung me an hour later. I all but ran down the road with Mickey pursuing, baying horribly, only by this time I had got the idea: he was all noise.

Was I sorry I had got myself into this? Yes, very. Was I going to shove it all in McLeod's hideous face and put up with Gloria and her twin, Mother? Not if I wanted to get up and out in the fall.

I felt like a mouse in a trap.

CHAPTER 4

You MIGHT SAY that all the things that happened, leading up to that terrible night in late August, fell into three stages. The next few weeks, when nothing too much seemed to happen except my going to McLeod's house every day and lugging back homework, was the first stage.

It was all very quiet. Even Gloria didn't give me her usual flak, being, at the time, occupied with her new boyfriend, Percy Minton (if you would believe the name), and was arrayed on the beach or down at the dinghy pier every day during those crucial hours of homework till I was sprung for the day at about three thirty.

Mother maintained a kind of hostile silence. She didn't know where I was, of course, in the early mornings. And for the first time in my life I was grateful that, if the world is divided into larks and nightingales as Barry Rumble Seat says, then Mother is definitely a nightingale. She may be up, that is, her body may be in a vertical position, as early as seven or eight, but she doesn't get assembled before about eleven. So if she were in the kitchen having some coffee or puttering in a vague way when I came back into the house from McLeod's, she'd probably say nothing at all, assuming I had been out on the beach or pier with the kids. When she did ask, I'd simply say, "Around," and she'd usually accept that, because one of the good things about today is that we have the older generation thoroughly housebroken. If they get too nosy you can drag in words like "authoritarian" and "over-compensatory" and they're so well trained by TV and all those articles in magazines about adolescents and Dr. Spock that they immediately begin to feel inadequate. They know right away they're doing something wrong.

Every now and then, of course, some deep instinct in Mother wells to the surface and she forgets all her good training and eays, "Where?"

That's when I say, "Down at the pier," or "At the boathouse," or something like that.

Once, out of some atavistic impulse, she pointed to the books under my arm and said, "With those books?"

"Is there any reason why I can't have quiet and fresh air the same time as I study?" I asked, putting a lot of "wronged victim" in my voice. I saw then that if I went upstairs and stayed for three hours in the unfresh air she'd figure something was fishy, so I moved immediately onto the offensive. "Gosh," I said, heading towards the back stairs, "You can see why kids take to drugs, it's about the only place they can get away from being asked questions like it's the FBI on your tail," and I absently scratched the inside of one elbow.

"Let me see your arm." There was so much panic in Mother's voice that I wanted to laugh, but I also felt a bit sorry.

"I'm clean!" I shoved up the sleeves of my sweat shirt. "Okay?"

She stared and slowly let out her breath. Then she

did a funny thing. She put her hands on my shoulders. "Chuck, I'm so frightened for you. How can I make you understand that whatever is the matter, taking a pill or a shot or anything like that will only make it worse. Please don't. Please."

I was hot and uncomfortable and wanted to get away.

"Look, what's the big deal about? Why all the drama? I'm not planning to turn on."

Suddenly she sat down. "All right."

For a minute there, I almost went back to the table. But sooner or later Gloria would come in, and whatever was going on between Mother and me she'd break up. Also, and this finally moved me upstairs, Mother is like me, not too bright, but Gloria would take one look at my books and I'd be fighting a rearguard action all the way up to my room. The answers that I could intimidate Mother into swallowing wouldn't go over with Sister Gloria for one second.

Of course Meg knew where I was going, but I was, tentatively of course, beginning to trust her. Once, when we passed each other on the beach and there was no danger of anyone overhearing, she asked me, "How's The Man Without a Face?"

"Gruesome."

"But is he going to get you through the exams?"

"Yes. I may be dead or nuts from brain-strain, but I'll pass."

Funny, until I walked on and was halfway along the beach I didn't realize that I had no doubt that McLeod would, somehow, force me through those entrance exams.

I joined a bunch of kids at the pier.

"Where ya been?" they asked.

"Around."

"Yeah? Around where?"

It was the same question as Mother's, but this time I knew where I was.

"The mainland."

"What's on the mainland?"

I put a smirk on my face. "Nothin' for you guys."

It's an updated version of the Tom Sawyer technique but it still works. Of course if there were anybody halfway smart enough they'd know it for a bluff and call it. The whole thing is not to let them have enough time to think. I jumped into one of the bigger dinghies that my family rented for the summer. "Anybody want to go up to the cove for a swim?"

For the time being I had the questions shelved. The cove was forbidden by all the authorities—the state, the township, the boat club, and the parents. Two kids had been drowned there in the past five years because of some kind of undertow, and a Coast Guard ship patrols the whole area during the summer. If any kid was caught there, his family was fined heavily, so the parents had a double reason for putting the cove out of bounds.

Naturally, we all went there. For one thing we could skinnydip, and anybody knows that that's a heck of a lot better than being all tractioned up in trunks.

Of course if I'd used my head I would have known that I couldn't go on telling Mother one thing and the kids another forever. Everybody talks to everybody; all the kids' parents knew Mother. Sooner or later adding-up time would come and I'd be in a mess.

Meg saw it and told me so.

One morning around dawn, which seems to be her favorite time for conversation, she came in and shook me awake and politely asked Moxie if she could sit down. By this time I suppose Moxie had, in his way, decided that she was okay, because while you couldn't say he was a one-cat welcoming committee, he didn't move when she plunked herself down on the bed. And if Meg sits on a bed you're in, you know it. Light she isn't.

"Why don't you go on a diet?" I said, not too pleased to be waked up.

"Don't make personal remarks. It's rude."

"Big deal."

She sighed. "I hate being fat. The whole *Zeitgeist* is against it."

That was another of The Hairball's favorite words. Being reminded of him at that hour just added insult. "Then why don't you stop stuffing something in your mouth every time you open it." I knew then I was sounding just like Gloria. "What is it you wanted to say?"

But Meg just sat there in her white nightgown not looking at me. Two big tears rolled down her cheeks.

I felt terrible. I didn't even know I could feel that way. I thought afterwards how I could have told her how I liked her, fat or no fat, and maybe put my arm around her or something. But all I could think of at that moment was what a slob I'd been making her cry, particularly since she was the only member of the family that gave a hoot about me.

"C'mon, Meg, I'm sorry. Don't cry."

She wiped her face and nose on the end of her nightgown. "It doesn't matter," she said, and of course she was lying.

"I like you a heck of a lot more than I like Gloria."

"That's not saying much." It wasn't.

"What did you come about?"

"That you'd better think up a good parent-and-gossip-proof reason for being on the mainland every morning and for having lied about it to Mother."

"Why? What's happened?"

Meg gave a sniff. "Do you have a Kleenex?"

"There're some in the drawer over there."

She got up, got a fistful, and got back on the bed. "Nothing's happened so far. But it's only a matter of time. The kids think you go to the mainland to smoke pot and Mother thinks you're studying under the trees. At the moment Gloria's not interested in you. But I think Percy's beginning to get restless, and if he gets away, then you know what'll happen: Gloria will give you her FULL attention."

"Why can't she hang onto her boyfriends, then she'd stay out of my life. I wish she'd elope or get married. But any guy who'd do that with her would have to have a death wish."

"If she could get him hooked—I mean signed, sealed and delivered with ring and everything— within the first weeks or couple of months of his falling in love with her, then she'd be okay. The trouble is, after that they start wanting out. It happened with Steve and Pete and Bill and Mike. And that just covers two summers."

It was true. Gloria in a bikini is one of the great scenic attractions of the Northeastern Seaboard. There was even a rumor that she was in the pay of the local chamber of commerce but I never fully bought that. Personally, I think she ought to wear something a little more subtle than two Band-Aids and an eye-patch, but I don't want to be called a square, so I hadn't said anything before. Now I said, "I wish she wouldn't strut around so naked. Why doesn't Mother stop her?"

"Because she can't. And if she tried, there'd be an awful row. Besides—Mother looks pretty good in a bikini herself."

"What's that got to do with it?" But the moment I said that I knew that in some way it had a lot to do with it.

"Mother likes to think of Gloria as herself."

"You're out of your skull!" I said angrily. "Gloria's mean. Mother isn't—at least, by herself she isn't. Just when Gloria's around."

"Yes. I know."

There was such a sad note in Meg's voice that I saw that while I thought I was always odd man out, she thought she was, too. "Why does she like Gloria better than us?"

"I don't know. Maybe with me because I'm fat."

"C'mon, Megsy. You know that's not so. Besides, I'm not fat and she doesn't like me any better."

"True." I could almost feel Meg brightening up a little. And I wanted to get off the subject of Mother. "Anyway, Barry Rumble Seat thinks you're great."

Meg perked up even more. "Yes. He does. And I like him. I wish Mother would marry him."

At that I did laugh aloud. "Barry's not her type. Not brainy enough."

"Shh!" Meg said. "Do you want Mother or Gloria in here? And Barry has *plenty* of brains. He just doesn't go around showing how intellectual he is. And he'd be very good for you, Chuck, if he did become our stepfather."

"I don't need a stepfather and I don't want one. I've had enough already." I don't know why what she said made me angry, but I could feel it inside me. "Look, it's getting light. I have go soon because McLeod likes to start on the button, and I don't want anybody awake when I leave. So far I've been able to get out without that. Maybe you'd better get back to your room."

"All right."

She got up and went to the door. Just before she opened it she turned. "What about McLeod?" she whispered. "For Mother."

"Are you crazy, Meg? You've got to be kidding.

Have you taken a good look at him? Can you see Mother wanting to—well, you know what I mean?"

Meg sighed. "No, I suppose not. Sometimes I think it's a pity we weren't born blind."

"What do mean by that? Who'd want to be born blind?"

"If we were *born* that way, we wouldn't know any different so we wouldn't feel deprived. Then everybody wouldn't always judge everybody else by the way they look."

She opened the door, peered around, and then slipped out.

It was a novel thought, and I pondered it on the way up to McLeod's house. I hadn't been able to get back to sleep, what with thinking over what Meg had said, and Moxie wanting some concentrated affection and communication before he slipped through the window, so I left earlier than usual, and arrived up at McLeod's house about a quarter to eight.

Usually, when I walked into the room we always worked in, he was there. This morning he wasn't. He wasn't in the barn, either, because I went and looked. Since the horse stall was empty, too, I guessed he was still out riding. He'd kept me so busy that I hadn't asked about the horse, or anything else. It was work, work, work. I always had the feeling that if I said anything personal at all, like *What do you do the rest of the time?* or *Is it true you write porno?* or even *Did you teach?* (he'd never even answered that one, or maybe I hadn't put it in the form of a question. Besides, who needed to ask?)—he'd toss me out. I knew he was telling the truth when he said he was sorry he'd got into this, because he made it perfectly obvious that if I put one toe over some kind of invisible line he'd drawn—such as not doing any of the whacking big assignments he'd dole out, or saying casually "Aeneas sure was a pompous ass"—I'd just get one of his chilling stares as though I had done something socially unacceptable. Because of the lousy exam, but also not to give him the satisfaction of getting rid of me, I kept on my side of the line, which meant keeping my mouth shut. Which was a pity, in a way, and a waste, because over the years I had really perfected the technique of how to keep a teacher from coming to grips with the fact that you haven't done your homework or don't know the answer to the question he's asking you.

In the school I go to it's considered repressive and damaging to the personality for a teacher not to pick up any subject a kid introduces. So if you don't know the correct dates of the Civil War, say, you just let on that you can't get your mind off the industrial ravages to the ecology or the terrible inequities of the electoral system or the racist nature of education or the Vietnam War or something like that, and if you have any skill at all you'll probably never have to feed him back the Civil War dates. One girl got so overwrought and convincing over dates representing an authoritarian approach to education that the teacher never mentioned them again. Some of the really hip kids have managed to carry it right through graduation, after which, of course (and if they know they'll blow their Regents) they drop out as a protest against the Establishment. There was only one teacher who didn't go along with that and who was crass enough to keep at you until it finally became evident that you hadn't a clue as to what he was talking about, hadn't read the assignment and couldn't hack his questions. So we had a secret meeting of the student body, after which the kids produced symptoms of such mass neurosis when they got home that the parents held their own emergency meeting and all but marched on the school. The teacher was fired.

But Monster McLeod obviously went by the old fascist methods, and since he had me where it hurts and St. Matthew's apparently really cared how much you knew about that pietistic ass Aeneas and his soggy girl friend, Dido, who kept reminding me more and more of Mother when she wants me to do something, I knew I had to live with it.

But to get back to that morning, I poked around the barn, looking at some of the harness on the wall and breathing in the smells of hay and horse and leather. There was a ladder going up to the upper part so I went up and waded around in the hay. It was really cool. I lay down and rolled like a puppy. The hay tickled my nose and my mouth and my midriff where my shirt rolled up. Then I got up and plunged around to another side and looked through a low square window with open shutters. It was a much better view than from the house. From here the village far below and to the right, the dinghy pier, the beach, and beyond, the rocks where the pines and spruce came right down to the water. It was beautiful and peaceful. After a while I lay down on my stomach in the hay and stared through the window. The air, which was fresher and cooler than down around our house, came in smelling salty. I put my hands under my chin and closed my eyes to see if I could smell both salt and hay at the same time. . . .

I had decided to go for a ride on McLeod's horse and was about to put a saddle on him when I noticed several things: he was about four times the size of any ordinary horse—more like an elephant, his ears rising above the stall were getting larger and larger, eyes were bright red, and he was going to kill me. To achieve that he was backing me into a corner, neighing wildly and rearing and shoving me in the side with his hooves. I was terrified but also puzzled as to why I wasn't already dead, because his hooves, which were like blades, kept coming at me, but instead of slicing off the top of my head, they merely nudged me in the ribs, like mitts. Then I got really frightened, because that stinking horse bared his teeth and *spoke*, just like that putrid commercial. It said in McLeod's voice,

"Wake up, Charles."

I opened my eyes. McLeod was standing over me. "Sorry to disturb you," he said drily.

I couldn't think what he was doing in my bedroom and was wondering how I could smuggle him out of the house without Mother or Gloria seeing him when he said, with equal sarcasm,

"Whenever you're ready."

I sat up, saw the hay, and then felt like a fool. McLeod moved around the loft, stepped to the edge, put his hand on it and vaulted down. Neat. I started to follow.

He looked up. "Use the ladder."

But of course I didn't. My landing left a lot to be desired. I fell on my back and knocked the wind right out of me. It was awful. I felt like I was drowning. I couldn't get in a breath. Dimly I saw McLeod turn, look at me and then come back on the double. He picked me up, bent me over, and started pounding on my back. Suddenly I could breathe.

"Are you all right?" he asked as I stood up, drawing in great gulps of air.

I nodded.

"You seem to have a mania for picking the one way of doing anything that will get you in trouble. Next time do what I tell you."

"Yes." I didn't feel up to arguing.

"All right, come on. I can't get Richard in here until you get out."

We started walking out. "What do you mean?" I asked, and saw the empty stall as I passed it.

"What I say. When I led Richard in here he started going berserk. Neighed and reared and tried to pull the reins out of my hand."

"So that's what I heard! I mean I was dreaming I was in the stall with Richard and he was rearing and neighing and trying to kill me." My head was beginning to clear. "You mean that even though I was upstairs in the middle of all that hay he knew I was there?"

"That's not unusual. A horse won't go over an unsafe bridge even though it looks perfectly all right to his rider. You know that."

"But what spooked him?"

"He's been abused. All people spook him, as you put it."

I had stopped short of the door. "But he's all right with you."

"Now he is. It took me weeks to get near him without his trying to stampede or shy, and more weeks to mount him."

"Did you know he was that way when you bought him?"

"Of course."

"Is that why you bought him?" I was galloping ahead with my questions to get as much as I could of this new slant on McLeod. I thought it would be hard to imagine him gentling a frightened animal but to my surprise, it wasn't. And of course, the moment I came to that conclusion, he clammed up.

"I think that's enough of the press conference this morning. You've managed to delay your lesson for half an hour so you should not feel it's been in vain."

But I wasn't entirely finished. "Is that how you knew I was up there?"

"It seemed a logical deduction."

He said it so drily I wanted to laugh. As we stepped from the dark stable into the sunlight I glanced up at him. At that moment he was looking down at me, smiling slightly. It was a nice smile, but I got the full benefit of his burned side. I looked away.

"Go back to the house and start translating where you left off."

His voice this time was different—so cold I wondered if he had seen me look away from him. I glanced back at him and for a second, just before he turned his face and walked off, I knew he had seen how I felt.

I watched him go over to a tree where he had tied Richard, then I went back to the house and opened up Vergil, wishing he hadn't seen my reaction quite so plainly. I was a little surprised, too, because one of the compensations of having a stupid look has always been that no one could tell what I was thinking. It used to drive The Hairball back up the tree, because all his students used to tell him how perceptive he was. He'd come home and have his ego inflated a little more by Mother and Gloria, and then he'd turn his radar equipment on me. And I'd just look at him as though he were talking Choctaw and bounce those waves right back at him.

But McLeod was not The Hairball. In fact, I found him puzzling. When he came back in the house it was as though we were back to square one, Vergil on ice, and that's the way it went for the next week or so. Every now and then he'd say something dry and funny and I'd laugh, and for a minute there we'd be on the same wavelength. I liked him then, I liked him a lot. Then bang! Out of the blue he'd freeze and I'd be back in the tundra.

"Do you like him?" Meg asked in one of our dawn's-early-light conversations.

By this time Moxie had accepted Meg as a blood relative and was purring as she ran a finger up and down his spine.

"Yes," I said, rather grudgingly. "He's okay—at least some of the time." It was funny, but not even to Meg did I want to say how I felt.

"What's he like?"

You can see now why I find females tiresome. That's a very female kind of question. "How the blazes do I know what he's like? That's a stupid question."

Meg didn't say anything, which I always find suspicious in women. It usually means they've decided to try for another opening.

I was right. Meg said, "Does he like you?"

"Will you cut out the inquisition? What are you anyway—the FBI?"

Still, it was an interesting question, and one to which I hadn't given any thought. I mean, I'm usually more interested in what I think of people than what they think about me, barring, of course, crucial types like Mother and Gloria where the answer has great bearing on how comfortable I am. Even my stepfathers didn't trigger me that way. For one thing, I came as a kind of package deal with Mother, which reduced the alternatives: they had to like me—or pretend to. For another, I didn't care. Besides, if you're an adolescent, it's a real challenge to get any member of the older generation to admit to plain not liking you. It's against their principles. For real! You can sweat out weeks of thought on how you can most bug an adult and come up with something really new and gross, and all you'll get is understanding. The hairier the act the more you're called an idealist reacting to an unresponsive society. I mean, it's frustrating. Joey swears he knows a boy who was so mad when he was asked (politely) to take the garbage out, that he emptied it instead—coffee grounds, melted Jell-O, baby's upchuck and everything—right on the new living-room carpet before God and everybody. The first thing that happened was that his father apologized for having been so insensitive to his needs. His mother burst into tears and said it was all her fault, and the next day he got the new bicycle he'd been hankering for. So why bother?

But no imagining could produce an image of Mc-Leod looking apologetic or guilt-ridden. All I could summon up was that chilling stare that left me in no doubt as to who would shortly be behind the eight ball, and the dry half-smile that vanished so quickly that day in the stable. No, I decided, he couldn't like me. In fact, he must hate me. The thought made me oddly unhappy.

I must have been thinking about it the next day as we struggled through some awful diatribe by Words-worth drooling over a half-witted child named Lucy, because McLeod put down the books and said, "If my face bothers you that much you can sit at the table over there by the window."

I realized then that I had been staring at him, and I could feel my own face get hot.

"I—it doesn't b-bother me. I mean—I'm s-sorry . . . I d-didn't—" Embarrassment won out. I couldn't go on.

He got up and ambled over to the window, his hands in his pockets. There was an awful silence. Here I go, I thought. Out. But it just goes to show that you should never say never, or think that just because your imagination boggles at something it can't happen.

McLeod said, "I'm sorry. I shouldn't have said that. Finish your comment about the poem."

I must have been really unstrung. What I wanted to do was to tell him somehow that I wasn't even think-ing about his face, although I could see, with me look-ing at him and away again, off and on like that, why he would think so. I tried to get my thoughts back to Lucy, hardly a mind-gripper under the best of cir-cumstances. But I couldn't concentrate.

"Well?"

"Your face doesn't bother me," I blurted out, and realized as I said it that it was true. I hadn't even thought about his disfigurement since that day in the stable. "I don't think about it that way any more."

He was sitting on the sill of the window, staring down at his crossed feet. "Then what were you thinking?"

I wanted to tell him but I didn't know how. I mean, I have pretty well perfected the techniques of how to put somebody down or off or out. But I didn't know how to begin to tell him that I was wondering whether or not he liked me, because that was like telling him that I liked him. It's disconcerting, making important discoveries like that in the middle of a conversation. Everything stops while I sort things out. One thing was certain: I'd never before tried to tell anyone— least of all a grown-up—that I liked him. The words were piling up in the back of my throat until I could almost feel my eyes bulge. But nothing came out.

"Never mind. I didn't mean to invade your privacy. Continue with Lucy." He came back to the table and stood looking down at his copy.

I was really in a turmoil, as though somebody had switched on a propeller somewhere in my midriff. Not knowing what to say, or rather, not knowing how to say what I wanted to say, I looked down at the book and grumbled, "The way he goes on about Lucy, it's worse than Humbert Humbert over Lolita. I mean—"

But I never got to what I meant.

There was an explosion of laughter. "Oh, my God," McLeod said and put his hand up to his eyes.

I felt rather clever. "It's crap, isn't it?"

I knew right away I'd gone too far, even though I could tell he still wanted to laugh. I said hastily, "I mean—the whole Lucy thing's silly, don't you think?"

"No. But it's a bad choice for you now at this age. They should know better. By the way, try for a word other than 'crap.' "

"It's a legitimate expression of authentic feeling," I quoted The Hairball piously.

"It's also laziness. When you have found ten syn-
onyms or reasonable substitutes then you may use it.
In the meantime, as part of your assignment tomorrow,
you can look up the Latin equivalents—there are
several—and decline them; then you can see how
they are used, in the Vergil."

I was furious. "That's a lot of work. Besides, you've
already set the homework."

"But a limited vocabulary is a serious handicap. I
should dislike your going to St. Matthew's under such
a grave disadvantage."

I stared back at him, too mad now to remember my
embarrassment. I knew good and well he was laughing at me, but not by a flicker did it show.

"By the way," he said. "Who were you quoting just
now?"

"The Hairball," I said, not thinking.

"The *what?*"

"My last stepfather."

"How many have you had?"

"Two. Then there was Mother's first husband who
would have been a step if I had been born then. Only
I wasn't. He was Gorgeous Gloria's father."

"The one you're so devoted to."

I decided to live dangerously. "I thought you were
never supposed to end a sentence with a preposition."

"I, too, can quote," he said deadpan. "There is a
certain type of insubordination going on around here
up with which I will not put."

I couldn't help grinning. "You're not serious about
me having to do that Latin word bit, are you, Mr.
McLeod?" (At our school in New York the teachers
all make a big thing about us calling them by their
first names. Democracy and all that. It didn't even
occur to me to try it with McLeod.)

"Oh, yes. That is, if you want to use your favorite
word again."

I sighed loudly. It really is against my principles to

give in to an adult. But somehow, of the two of us, I had a strong feeling he wasn't going to do the yielding.

"All right. I won't—at least, I'll try to remember."

"Angels could no more," McLeod said, moving towards the bookcase.

I gathered my things up. "Is that from a poem?"

"Yes."

"That stuff always turns me off."

He pulled down a volume. "You like planes, don't you?"

"Sure."

He came back, turning over the pages. "You might like this," he said, and read aloud:

> Oh, I have slipped the surly bonds of earth,
> And danced the skies on laughter-silvered wings;
> Sunward I've climbed and joined the tumbling
>   mirth
> Of sun-split clouds—and done a hundred things
> You have not dreamed of—wheeled and soared
>   and swung
> High in the sunlit silence. Hov'ring there,
> I've chased the shouting wind along and flung
> My eager craft through footless halls of air.
> Up, up the long delirious, burning blue
> I've topped the wind-swept heights with easy
>   grace,
> Where never lark, or even eagle, flew,
> And, while with silent, lifting mind I've trod
> The high untrespassed sanctity of space,
> Put out my hand, and touched the face of God.

It was queer, what it did to me. There were little explosions in my head and stomach and a tingling down my back. My throat was dry. McLeod was looking at me. "Here," he said, holding out the book. "Take it."

CHAPTER 5

IT WAS AFTER TWELVE when I got home. McLeod had kept me half an hour overtime, although, come to think of it, I hadn't felt kept. I just hadn't realized it was so late. But I did realize I was hungry. The house was blessedly empty. I like empty houses or rooms. I once said this to one of the five school psychologists and he got so upset that they broke out a fresh set of Rorschachs for me to run through. So I went through all their bags of tricks and answered all their stupid questions and I still like empty houses and rooms, especially those that are empty of people I'm related to, except maybe Meg.

Feeling relaxed and eager to look at that poem again, I was pouring myself some milk when the screen door squeaked open and in came Gorgeous Gloria and Putrid Percy.

"Hi," Gloria said, oozing with friendship. Then she gave me a big smile and I knew instantly what all our roles were: hers was The People's Choice as Big Sister of the Year. Mine was the same as it always is, Unappreciative Kid Brother. Mother's is Unappreciative Parent. Meg's is Unappreciative Kid Sister. The plot is whatever is happening at the moment. But I was the only member of the cast available, which meant that the burden of revealing the Unappreciation by which Gloria is always surrounded lay solely, and heavily, on me. I watched her carefully over the glass of milk I was drinking to see how the plot developed.

"Percy, this is my kid brother, Chuck."

He tossed his head to get a long curling lock out of the way. "Hi, man."

I waved a hand. "Hi," I said, when I had finished drinking the milk.

Gloria glanced at the books that I had put down on the table. "Chuck's trying to get into St. Matthew's," she explained in a kindly fashion.

Percy took a bite out of a doughnut Gloria had taken out of a jar. "Anybody can do that," he mumbled through a full mouth, showing a lot of teeth and wet dough. Then he swallowed. "What's your problem, man?"

"Chuck's not the academic type," Gloria said, nibbling at a carrot stick, and still eyeing the books.

My part was beginning to shape up. I was now not only Unappreciative Brother, I was also Backward Brother.

"Percy goes to Princeton," Gloria said (as if we all didn't know), turning the top book around so she could see the title on the spine.

I suddenly realized that was McLeod's book, and for all I knew he might have his name in it, and then Gloria would really have a plot to get to work on.

I'm not usually a fast thinker. But Gloria's hand was on the cover of the book about to open it, and emergency bells were clanging in my head. There wasn't time to put the milk container I was holding down or back in the refrigerator, so I dropped it.

Milk flew all over the floor and over Gloria's feet. The People's Choice for Big Sister vanished as the real

Gloria stood up. "You clumsy clot," she shrieked in her best witchlike voice. "You verminous moron. You did that deliberately."

"Gosh, I'm sorry." I tucked the books under my arm and moved towards the back stairs. "But if you get it off right away everybody says it won't stain." I opened the door to the stairs.

Percy the Pursuer was slapping at his shorts with a rag. "Lousy coordination," he was muttering. But he was looking in a strange way at Gloria, and who could blame him? America's sweetheart, voice like an ungreased axle, was enumerating the goodies in store for me once Mother had been apprised of my latest sin.

"You did that deliberately," she said, staring up from the floor where she was wiping off her sandals. "I know you, Chuck Norstadt, that's your subtle way of distracting my attention. You've done it before. And don't think I won't find out what it is you don't want me to know and tell Mother. I will, I always do, and then you'll be so sorry you'll *crawl*."

I really couldn't have written her part better myself, if the object was to show Percy what he was about to take to his heart, if not home. Which just goes to prove what everybody says: I'm not very bright. If I had been, I would have given my all to convince Percy what a jewel he was about to acquire. With any luck they'd elope—at the least he'd keep her attention occupied. Instead, I couldn't have done a more efficient job of showing her up if I'd planned it for a week.

Her voice followed me up the stairs. I closed my door and stuck a chair under it—there isn't a key in the house, and in this mood Gloria wouldn't hesitate to walk in. Then I sat down at the small table that serves me for a desk and cursed my idiocy. It was the big sister bit that got me—of all her acts it's the most repulsive. When she's being her real self it's unpleasant, but nobody's fooling anybody else. It's the phoniness that brings out the worst.

I looked down at McLeod's book and flipped open the front cover and there, sure enough, was his name: Justin McLeod. Then I nearly fell over because underneath his name was *St. Matthew's School.* And then there was a date, 1958.

I did some hasty figuring. He certainly couldn't have been a student in 1958, that was only thirteen years ago, so he must have been a teacher.

I racked my memory for what he had said about the school—nothing really, except at the beginning when he implied it shouldn't be too hard to get in.

But the real mystery was—why hadn't he said he had been there?

I riffled through the pages and found the poem again. It was called "High Flight," and it was by somebody named John Gillespie Magee. And even just reading it, without McLeod's voice, which was good, it had the same effect. That Magee really knew about flying. I've been up in a small one-engined plane twice. Nobody knew about it either. I just took some money out of my savings, got on the Long Island train when I should have been at school, and went over to a private airport on the Island. Those were the two best days I ever had.

An hour or so later there was a banging on my bedroom door. "It's me," Meg said. I got up and let her in.

"Now you've done it," she said gloomily. "Charles—you just aren't very smart."

"What else is new?" I said sarcastically.

"What happened?" She flopped down on the bed, sand and all.

"What d'ya mean, what's happened?" I sounded surly, but my heart sank.

"I mean I was playing down at the cove with some of the other kids when I looked up, and there was our Gloria with a double-dip chocolate-chip-marshmallow ice cream cone which she said was for me. So I knew she wanted something."

"So of course you refused it—the ice cream cone, I mean."

"No," Meg said sadly.

"Maybe you aren't so bright, either."

"*D'accord.*" Meg's pretty conceited about her French which she jabbers with Barry Rumble Seat who spent some years in Paris.

"Whatever that means."

"It means right on."

"What did Gloria want?"

"She wanted to know, casual-like, if you were studying with anyone and if so, who."

"Whom." McLeod's iron approach to grammar was beginning to have effect.

"Boy! He must be good if he got that through your head."

"Thanks a lot! He is. What did you tell her, Meg?"

"I told her that you were studying by yourself but had discovered some morning hideout where you can have peace and quiet. But I don't think she believed me."

"Who would, since you go lobster red every time you try and tell a lie."

"I can't help it. Is it my fault if I'm naturally honest?"

"You might remember it's in a good cause."

"That has nothing to do with it. She also said that one of your books didn't look like any book she'd seen around the house before and whose was it?"

"Well that just proves what I've always thought—that she goes snooping around my room when I'm not there. How the heck does she know which is my book and which isn't? Whose did you say it was?"

"I told her I thought it was Pete Lansing's."

Good old Pete, I thought. First his jeans and now his book. "Did she swallow it?"

"I don't think so, and neither would I if I'd known what kind of book it was; she said it was hard to imagine Pete having a poetry anthology."

I remembered her turning the book around and squinting at the title. "Lousy peeping tom," I muttered.

"I said it could have been given to him."

"Thanks, Meg, that was neat."

"I thought so too. But all the same, she'll check. Look—I've been thinking all the way up here. Is there any way you could study up at McLeod's house? That'd solve a lot of problems. You could keep your books up there so Gloria could snoop to her heart's content. Mother already thinks you're breathing the great outdoors, and if you were just up there out of the way who'd know the difference?"

"McLeod."

"Would he care?"

"Yes. He can hardly wait to get me out of there in the mornings."

"You mean he really dislikes you that much?"

There we went again. Same old question. "How the heck should I know?"

"Okay, okay. Keep your shirt on." She got up. A lot of sand detached itself and fell onto the rug. "I don't know why you have to get so het up."

"Because I can't see him letting me stay up there and study. But if I don't Gloria will find out somehow sooner or later, because I use a lot of his books now. And then Mother'll know and—"

"Ask him," Meg said firmly. "What can you lose?"

I knew the answer to that without thinking. "Everything." I paused. "You're always asking if he likes me. Well, sometimes I think he does, and sometimes I don't. But I sure don't want to rock the boat trying to find out. And me asking him to let me study up there—which would be six hours in his house altogether—might be all he needs to say the deal is off."

"Why?"

"I don't know why. It's just a hunch. Maybe because he'll want to know why and if he finds out Mother doesn't know I'm up there I've got a feeling he'll blow the works. He's the kind of guy who likes things shipshape and kosher."

"He doesn't know you haven't told Mother you're studying with him?"

"I don't think so. I haven't exactly said so, but he's pretty sharp."

I was silent. The old feeling of being painted into a corner was getting to me again.

"Cast yourself on his mercy," Meg said dramatically.

"Do you have to be so corny?"

"All right. What's the alternative?"

She had me there.

I suppose I could have waited until the next morning to return the poetry anthology. But I wouldn't have had any peace. I could hardly stay in my room all day, nor could I keep watch on Gloria. I thought about hiding the book, but the great question was, where? The house was a slung-together summer cottage with a minimum of everything, including storage space. With McLeod's name in it I couldn't take any risk. So, along with another of his books, a history text (but without his name in it), I started the long climb up to his house.

When I got there I didn't know quite what do do. Normally, if this were the morning, I'd just open the front door and walk in. But this wasn't morning. which made me into something else—an uninvited visitor. I was sort of hoping he might not be there. I could then simply leave the books on the porch away from where they could get rained on. But sooner or later I'd have to tell him about the situation and leaving him to find the books he'd lent me without any explanation would give him plenty of time to wonder what I was doing back on his property and get mad about it.

So, I took the cautious approach and rang the bell.

In a minute McLeod opened the door. "What's up?" He saw the books. "Such promptness! You could have brought them back tomorrow. There's no charge for the first twenty-four hours."

Funny man, I thought glumly.

"Something on your mind?"

I nodded.

"All right. Come in."

We went into the library. The reading light was on above the big leather chair. Beside it there was a sort of a chest. On it were a plate and a glass that looked as if it had had milk in it and an empty cup and saucer. Usually anything that reminds me of food makes me hungry, especially since I hadn't had lunch. But I was too nervous.

McLeod saw my glance. "Hungry?"

I shook my head. "No," I croaked, and then cleared my throat.

McLeod stood with his back to the empty fireplace, feet slightly apart, hands behind his back. He looked about a foot taller than usual. I wished I had waited till morning.

"Well—out with it."

I had planned a sort of explanatory preamble and groped after the first sentence as though it were the end of a ball of twine. Nothing came.

McLeod started to frown. I knew that look of old, so I closed my eyes and plunged. "Could I study up here—please? I mean the three hours after the coaching?"

I had expected his usual flat "no," but he simply said, "Why?"

I had planned this, too, something about Mother having regular committee meetings or socials. But I knew right away it was no use. I took a breath.

"Mother doesn't know I'm coaching here with you. She doesn't really want me to go to St. Matthew's. Gloria saw your book today. If she opened it she'd see your name in it and she'd tell Mother."

"Why doesn't your mother want you to go to St. Matthew's?" The question came sharply.

"It's not St. Matthew's especially. It's like I told you that first night—she doesn't want me to go away."

"And if you told her she'd stop you?"

"Yes. Maybe. I'm not sure. Not by herself. But Gloria would brainwash her. She'd give her a lot of good reasons why I shouldn't."

"You seem to have a persecution mania about her. Either that or she's a little demented herself. Boys your age often have trouble with older sisters, but not like this. Why does she have such a vendetta against you?"

"I don't know. Mother once said—"

"What?"

"Well, it sounds screwy, but because I was born. Something about me taking not only her attention off Gloria, but also my father's."

"That could be. Infant girls often have fixations about their fathers."

"But he wasn't her father." The idea horrified me. "Besides, it doesn't make any sense. She's always so lousy about him. Calls him a dumb jock. She once even said—"

"What?"

But this was one of the things I didn't like to remember. I looked down and shook my head.

There was a silence. I could feel the air from the open window on my face and smell the sharp tang of the sea.

"All right," McLeod said. "But for what it's worth I think you're making a mistake."

"Why?"

"Not having it out with your mother."

"She wouldn't listen to me, I just told you. In the end she does what Gloria wants."

"Maybe. You put an awful lot on other people—your mother won't listen to you. Your sister hates you. Aren't you anything but a puppet being worked on by other people? Are you quite sure you can't get your mother to listen? Maybe you've talked yourself into that so you don't have to confront her."

"You mean I'm copping out?"

"Aren't you?"

I was so angry I stammered. "Th-that's not t-true."

"Then why don't you talk to her?"

The old feeling of being backed into a corner was coming over me and I wanted out. "I'll see you tomorrow," I said, and turned, making for the door. The heck with studying here. I'd find some other place.

"Charles."

I went on, pretending I hadn't heard.

"Charles! Come back here now or don't come back tomorrow or any other morning."

I stopped. After a minute I turned and went back because there was nothing else I could do. What on earth had made me think I could make McLeod do what I wanted? I stood in front of him, sullen, my eyes on the floor.

"Look at me."

I looked up and stared at the mangled half of his face.

"What are you afraid of?"

"I don't know. Nothing."

"Because whatever it is you'll have to meet it sooner or later." He added drily, "That could be called a universal law." And then, "Is it about your father?"

It all came back to me at that moment, as fresh and yeasty as though it were yesterday. It was the day on the beach three years ago when Gloria had called my father a dumb jock, and started to say something about my not knowing the truth about him. This was during one of our nastier fights after she had kicked over my sand castle and I had flattened her in the sand and rubbed a lot of it in her hair. She was about to go on about my father when Barry shoved a towel over her head—to get the sand out, he said—and bore her off. Mother swore up and down she didn't know what Gloria was talking about. So did Barry when I asked him later. I believed them. I had to.

"What is it?" McLeod asked.

"Nothing." I started to turn again, still hunting for the exit.

McLeod reached out and took my shoulder. "You can study here. That's what you want, isn't it?"

Curiously, I had forgotten. I nodded. "Okay. Thanks."

"It's all right. I'm sorry I gave you such a hard time." He dropped his hand. "I'm not used to people any more. I suppose I've grown surly and suspicious." He added abruptly, "Have you eaten?"

"No."

"Are you hungry?"

I suddenly discovered I was ravenous. I nodded. "Yes."

I was finishing off a hugh meat and cheese sandwich when McLeod, who was drinking some more coffee and walking restlessly around the kitchen, said, "Are you sure there's no reason—other than wanting you at home—that your mother doesn't want you to go to St. Matthew's? Is it financial?"

I swallowed the last bite and cleaned up a bit of mayonnaise with a piece of crust. "No. It's not financial. There's some kind of fund that sends us all to school." I put the crust in my mouth, chewed it and swallowed, and then remembered something. "Of course, there's what The Hairball said. He's not

Mother's husband any more, but maybe that's part of it."

"What did he say?" McLeod picked up my plate and glass and took them with his cup and saucer to the sink. I licked my fingers. "He seemed to think that all boarding schools were full of homos and if you weren't that way when you got there you soon would be."

There was a silence. Then McLeod turned on the water and I got up and started to shove my chair in.

After a minute McLeod turned off the water. "That's not true," he said. "It can crop up anywhere, including public schools. Most boarding schools are extremely careful about that kind of thing." He tore off a paper towel. "By the way. Do you have a current stepfather? I sometimes find them hard to keep up with."

I grinned. "You and me. No. But there probably will be. Mother doesn't like staying unmarried too long—" And it was then that Meg's idea about McLeod's being Mother's next husband came swimming back, making me stop in midsentence. It didn't seem such a crazy idea as when she mentioned it.

"That sounds like an unfinished sentence."

"No. Not really. I just thought of something."

He looked at me for a minute. "Is there a current candidate?"

Delighted he couldn't see what was really going on in my mind I said, "Only Barry Rumble Seat— but he's always around."

"Barry *who?*"

"Rumble Seat. His real name's Rumbolt."

McLeod had a funny look. Then he said, "How long have you known him?"

"I dunno—years, off and on."

"Does he know you're up here—that I'm coaching you?"

"No. Of course not."

McLeod went over and took a jacket off a hook near the back door.

"Do you know him?" I asked.

But I guess he didn't hear, because the screen door had swung to behind him. He waved. "See you tomorrow."

CHAPTER 6

MEG WAS RIGHT. Staying up there after the actual coaching took off a lot of the strain and made everything easier. I'd leave the house shortly after seven, which was no sweat since I'm an early riser. McLeod would work with me till eleven. Then I'd have some milk and cookies and a sandwich and was usually eating those when I heard him ride past on Richard. At that point I'd have to remind myself why I was there and what I was doing and whose idea it was in the first place, because getting back to studying while I could still hear Richard's hooves galloping back over the fields was almost more than I could bear. Sometimes McLeod wouldn't return till nearly two, quitting time. Sometimes he'd come back sooner, walk in and sit down with a book, all without saying a word. But if he was in the room it was almost like he wasn't there. I mean, normally I have to be alone to concentrate, but he didn't bother me. The first day when I got up to go out at two he said I'd better have something to eat, so we went out to the kitchen.

"There's stuff in the regrigerator. Make yourself a sandwich."

Usually after that we had sandwiches and milk or coffee. At first this happened only a couple of times a week. Other days I'd have a hot dog and a milkshake as soon as I got to the village. But then I got to staying up at McLeod's three or four times a week, then every day. Sometimes I'd ask him questions about what I'd been working on, although I was afraid at first that he'd think I was trying to scrounge more coaching out of him, but he didn't seem to. Then around two thirty or a quarter to three I'd wander down to the beach. Once or twice, when he was going to the village or back into the mainland, he drove me as far as the bridge.

The work got more interesting. What I really found I liked was history and next to that, math, which really rocked me. But it made me feel a lot better about the future, because Meg always said that with my math grades the whole system would have to go back to the Wright brothers before they'd let me in the Air Force Academy.

As the days went on I sometimes stayed later and later. One afternoon we got to talking in the kitchen. I found myself looking at the kitchen clock and it was five to five.

"It's got to be wrong," I said.

"What?"

"Your clock."

He turned and looked at it. "No, it's right, I wound it this morning."

I stood up so fast I knocked my chair over. "I didn't know it was s-so late."

McLeod got up. "If you're stricken because you took so much of my valuable time, don't be. My time isn't that sacred."

That made me think of something. "Is it true that you—"

Why, I mentally kicked myself, when things were going well, did I always have to ask some question that wasn't any of my business? If McLeod had made one thing clear above all others it was that he had a highly developed sense of privacy. It spread out like a moat around him. Every so often, like this afternoon, I would find myself inside it and then, instead of leaving well enough alone, I'd shove my whole leg in my mouth and start asking pointy little questions.

He was standing, hands on the back of his chair. "Is it true that I what?"

One thing I had learned: If you start something like the wrong question with McLeod you finish it, you don't just stop in the middle and leave by the nearest exit—not if you wanted to come back. I felt sick but I went on. "That you make your living writing porno under a pseudo-whatever-it-is?"

There was a second's pause. That's done it, I thought. Then he started to laugh and went right on as he picked up the dishes and put them in the sink.

I was so relieved I felt weak.

"Is that the current story?"

"Yes. It's all those packages and what look like checks from publishers."

"You mean our dedicated postmistress has been corrupted?"

I grinned. "No. At least I don't think so. But the word's around." I told him about the mass pilgrimage to the bookstores and he laughed even harder. At that moment he was warm and funny and almost young.

He finished washing the two dishes, glasses, and the cup and saucer. I dried them and put them away.

"It's not porno," he said finally. "It would be a lot more lucrative if it were."

"Novels?" Somehow he didn't seem the novel type, at least not the kind that Meg's father, the publisher, or The Hairball left lying around the house.

"Yes. In a sense. A mixture of science fiction and mythology."

"Under your name?"

"No. Terence Blake."

I whistled. "Wow!" The Terence Blake books hadn't yet caught on like Tolkien but they were really good. "That's great! I mean—your books are super!" I was impressed. What a pity I couldn't tell everybody, although the minute I thought of that I knew I didn't want to.

He smiled. "Sweet words to any author. Which ones have you read?"

I told him. "There're two earlier ones I haven't read. Somebody stole them from the school library and the bookstores say they're out of print. But they're coming out in paperback in the fall so I'll get 'em then."

"I have them. You can borrow them."

As we went towards the living room I said, "Why Terence Blake?"

"Terence was my father's name and Blake my mother's maiden name."

"But why a pseudonym? I mean—I'd be pretty proud if I'd written them."

"But when I wrote the first I had no idea how it would go."

Somehow I knew that wasn't the real reason, but I also knew I'd better not press it. He had that remote note in his voice. We went over to the bookshelves. He pulled down two books and handed them to me.

"Are they your only copies?" I asked.

"That's all right. I trust you."

I felt pretty good when he said that. But I shook my head.

"No. If anybody saw them they'd last about five minutes. Every kid on the beach would want them, and then they'd want to know how I'd got hold of them." Reluctantly, but feeling heroic, I handed them back. "When they come out in paper I'll send them to you to autograph. Would you? I mean autograph them?"

"Of course."

He said it so abruptly I wondered if I had put my foot in my mouth again. "You don't mind?"

He was putting the books back on the shelf, but he turned and looked at me. "No, Charles. I don't mind."

I remember that summer partly as pictures that spring into my mind, knife-sharp, partly as fragments of conversation.

Once he asked me, "What do you want most? Quickly—don't think."

"To be free."

"Free from what?"

"From being crowded. To do what I want."

"Fair enough. Just don't expect to be free from the consequences of what you do, while you're doing what you want."

At the time I was disappointed in McLeod. It sounded like some typical adult double-talk.

Another time, I was copying down the poem he read me, "High Flight," so I could put it in a note-book along with the other stuff about flying that I had been keeping off and on since I was about seven. I asked him if he believed in God.

"Of course." He said it almost impatiently.

I waited for him to ask what I thought, but he didn't. Then he saw my face and laughed. "What were you expecting? That I would proselytize you?"

I grinned, feeling foolish. His ability to read me was unnerving. "Well, The Hairball always said that was the trouble with True Believers—they had to spread the word."

"In a sense, he's right. But in your case it's time you reached out for what you want—instead of waiting for people to come after you."

"How do you mean?"

"About ninety percent of your time seems to have been spent resisting things and people, so that it's now an emotional habit. It's time you reached out on your own."

"I came here."

"Yes. Did you ever stop to think—if your mother or one of your numerous stepfathers had said, 'Charles, we've arranged for you to have coaching this summer. You'll be coached for three hours five days a week and then you'll spend an equal amount of time studying while your friends are down on the beach or out in boats, and as your reward you'll get into a school that you don't much want to go to but is the lesser of two evils,' how do you think you would have felt?"

He had a point. "Lousy."

Looked at that way six hours of studying and being coached sounded like the worst nightmare of sweat labor. I must be out of my mind. But the truth of the matter was that I was enjoying myself which, since I wasn't any shakes as a student even now, meant I was enjoying McLeod. He wasn't like anybody I had ever known. I finished copying the poem and read it over. According to the footnote the author, Magee, died at nineteen—killed during the Battle of Britain—in 1941 which, as far as I was concerned, was practically back in the American Revolution. But I started doing some calculations. What I was really trying to find out was whether McLeod had gotten burned as a pilot. The idea appealed to me. Anybody who was, say, nineteen in 1941 would be—I did some figuring on the edge of my paper—about fifty now. Possible. I looked up at McLeod who was rearranging some books on a shelf. The good side of his face was turned toward me so that I could see only a swatch of the burn coming around his chin. There was a lot of gray in his hair. On the other hand, some people got gray at thirty.

"What are you trying to figure out?" he asked, without turning.

Caught short I blurted out, "I was wondering how old you are."

"The easiest method is to ask. Forty-seven."

Some more figuring. But not even McLeod was fighting the Battle of Britain at sixteen. But he could have been an American Air Force pilot at the very end of the war. My heart started to beat faster. "Were you in the Air Corps during World War II?"

"No."

"You weren't in the war?"

"Yes. Infantry. A foot-slogging private soldier."

"Is that where you—" Asking about his age and asking about a burn that disfigured half his face was not exactly the same thing.

"Where I—?"

I wished I hadn't started. But I was still stinging from his comment about my tendency to run. "Where —where you got burned."

He was looking at me but his face didn't flicker. For the first time I wondered what it could be like for him. "I shouldn't have asked that," I mumbled.

"Most people do, sooner or later." He put another book on the shelf from a pile on the floor. "I got burned in a car accident." He paused and then added deliberately, "I was too drunk to know what I was doing, slid on some ice, and went over the side of the road down a ravine."

I was stunned. It sure knocked my picture of the wounded war hero to fragments. "I'm sorry," I said, not sure whether I was sorry he had lost his face or I had lost the war hero.

He was watching me. "So am I. Not just because of this—" he gestured to the burned half of his face

"—but because there was a boy with me, a boy about your age. He was burned to death."

A bee had somehow got in the room and was buzzing around. In the silence that followed it sounded like a 747.

Then McLeod said, "It's late, Charles. You'd better go."

The day after, I woke up before dawn, thinking about what McLeod had said. The queer part was that I expected to feel disgusted and disillusioned, and I didn't. I felt sorry. I felt sorry for the boy who was killed, but I felt more sorry for McLeod. It didn't make much sense because the boy was dead, but I was sure McLeod had been dragging around the guilt ever since, and that it had a lot to do with the way he lived and why he had never had his face fixed the way Mother and everyone in the summer community said he could—and should.

"What a lousy deal," I said to Moxie, who was lying under the sheet next to me. My voice must have waked him, because I felt suddenly the deep vibration against my ribs that meant he was purring. In a few seconds the noise followed, sounding like a bad case of bronchitis.

A while later Meg came into my room. Since I had a lot to think about I wasn't too pleased to see her.

"How is the Great Man?" she said, wiggling her backside against the footboard and crowding my feet.

"Okay." I didn't want to talk about McLeod.

"You're getting very protective about him."

"What's to talk about?"

"All right. Keep your hair on. But people are beginning to ask what you're doing all the time and where you are."

"And what do you tell them?"

"I tell the kids you're being forced to study with some teaching type on the mainland. And whenever

Mother says 'Where's Chuck?' which she does sometimes in the afternoons—she's resigned to your studying in the mornings—I say wherever your gang is at the moment, except when they're right there, then I make up something else. But one of these days she won't ask me, she'll ask Pete or Sam or Tom, and then the fat will be in the fire."

"And Gloria? What's with her?"

"She's still got a clutch on Peerless Percy. But Sue Robinson's coming here from camp next week."

"Yueh!" I struggled up and sat leaning against the headboard. "That's bad news." It was. Sue is Gloria's only real competition: red hair, green eyes, and if her figure isn't quite as nymphy as our Gloria's, her personality is several light-years better.

"And," Meg went on, as though winding up for a real knockout blow, "she was the one Peerless Percy was in love with all last summer."

Things did not look good. But somehow I didn't care. It all seemed remote and unimportant. My mind slid back to what McLeod had told me.

"You don't seem interested," Meg said.

"Sure I'm interested, Meg. But I've got other things to think about. Besides, I'm tired. I haven't slept much. I'd like to catch another hour's shut-eye before I have to get up. After all," I finished virtuously, "you may be having a vacation. I have to work."

"All right." Meg was made and I knew it.

"Don't be miffed, Megsy."

She turned. "You're different, Chuck. You've changed."

"What d'ya mean?"

"I don't know," Meg said slowly. "I can't say what I mean. But you're different. And I don't like it."

"Meg!"

But she was out of the room, and I was fairly sure she was crying. Well, I thought, getting back under the sheet, I'd make it up to her somehow. I knew she was kind of lonely because there weren't too many of her age group up here this year. Our summer community is very age-oriented. The grown-ups do their thing, which is mostly dropping in on each other for drinks or lying out at their end of the beach or back of one another's houses nursing their tans. Only the kids swim much. It's pretty rocky and the water's cold. Which is probably why I had gotten away with my double life for so long. Structure was a bad word around here and asking too many questions was showing definite signs of structure.

I comforted myself with this thought (Meg's forebodings had upset me more than I wanted to admit) and went to sleep thinking about McLeod, knowing there was something I had to say and hoping that when the moment came I'd say it properly.

He was remote and full of trick and trap questions later that morning, really grilling me as to what I had learned, not just lately, but right from the beginning. By the time the three hours were over I felt limp. He must have seen this because he brought some milk and cookies into the library immediately.

"You'd better go out and run for half an hour after you've eaten. I'd lend you Richard if he weren't so neurotic."

"How is he?" I asked, downing cookies at a great speed.

"All right."

"Look," I burst out. I was determined to have my say. "About what you told me yesterday. About the accident—" I kept my eyes on the table where I was nervously turning the cookie dish around and around. "What I want to say is—well, it was a lousy thing to happen to you, and it probably wasn't your fault."

"You're wrong. It most definitely was."

"All right. So it was. What I mean is—" I wanted so badly to tell him how I felt, but I couldn't find the words. Then a strange thing happened. Without my volition, my hand reached towards his arm and I grasped it.

He didn't move or say anything. The good half of his face was as white as paper. Then he jerked my hand off and walked out.

CHAPTER 7

I WAS SORE as a boil. Worse—I felt like a fool.

So. He thought I ought to reach out! What a hypocrite! Here I had been thinking he was something special in grown-ups, and he turned out to be like all the rest: say one thing, do another.

I was so mad I found it hard to concentrate. Even so, I couldn't get over the feeling there was a funny side to it. If this coaching had been Mother's—or the school's—idea, what an opportunity to walk out and say screw 'em. But it was mine, so I had to stay even though McLeod had acted like my hand was a cockroach or something. Like, for pete's sake, I had made a pass at him. That's what burned me up. Well—screw him! I'd take what I could from him, pass my exam, and then tell him to go to hell.

But fantasies of telling him to go shove didn't help me to concentrate. I stuck it out till around twelve thirty. At that point, having taken in about zero, I split.

As I was pelting down the path I heard Richard's hooves behind the long belt of pines on the other

side of the cliff, coming at a fast clip. I didn't want
to meet McLeod, so I put on a burst of speed, vaulted
over the gate, and high-tailed it to the bridge and
across. Then I left the main road and went down
the steep hill that gave onto the back of the village.
Once there I felt safe. I strolled to the outdoor counter
of the malt shop and treated myself to two hamburgers
and a double malt which, having paid for, I could only
eat half of. This morning was really a bomb!

From where I was standing I could see inside. A
whole lot of Gloria's gang were there, but I couldn't
see any of mine. So when I had eaten all I could, I
decided to pay the cove a visit.

Running down the pier I jumped into one of the
dinghies, untied it, and rowed past the point and
north along the coast until I hit the cove. One of the
reasons we had picked the cove was that from the sea-
ward side it looked more or less like any other string
of big rocks lining that part of the shore. But when
you got right up to one end where there was a narrow
opening, you could see the rocks were sort of a jetty
running parallel with the shore, shielding a small
beach in the elbow.

I turned in at the right place, rowed across the
tiny cove, and tied the dinghy to a tree stump near
the edge of the water. Then I ran around the curve,
dodged around a big boulder, and there they all were
—Pete Minton (Percy's brother), Sam Leggett, Tommy Klein, Luke and Mike Warner, and Matt Henry.
They were all stretched out except Pete, who was sitting with his back against a rock. Thin spirals of smoke
rose from each. Then I smelled it: pot.

—That was something I certainly hadn't bargained
for. There was always a lot of talk about getting some,
but grass in these parts is about as easy to find as porno.
But I couldn't go back now.

"Behold the grind!" Pete said dreamily.

"How's the studying going?" Mike asked.

"And how's the guy without a face?" Tommy pitched in. "What's his name, fellers?"

"McLeod," they all chorused.

So they knew. "Okay." I sat down and leaned against a tree. I was really shaken but didn't want to show it. I wanted very much to know how they knew, but knew better than to ask. Pulling a grass blade from near one of the rocks I smoothed it between my thumbs and blew it a couple of times, making a thin screeching noise.

"Man, you must really want to get into that funky school," Pete said.

"Haven't you heard, he wants to be a flyboy," Sam took a long drag on his joint. "Off we go, into the wild blue yond-der. . . ." He broke off into a giggle.

"Shove it," I said.

"So sorry, sir. *Achtung! Sieg heil!* Up yours!"

"I said shove it."

"My, aren't we sensitive? Who said you could come out here, anyway? You aren't one of us any more."

"Yeah? So who's gonna make me move?"

They were so bombed I felt pretty safe saying that, although even if they weren't I could take any of them on alone, even Pete, who's heavier than I am. None of them is exactly what you'd call athletic.

There were no takers, but I knew I was on very dicey territory. Somehow, I didn't know how, they knew what I doing and they'd read me out of the club. I lay back and thought about it. It didn't take a genius to arrive at the answer: Meg had meant well but they knew I wasn't being forced to study. If this had been Mother's or the school's idea I would have been down here every afternoon griping about it. What's more, it would have been the same time every day—the second school was out. That would have made it okay. I would have been just another victim of terrible parental and school pressure to achieve. It was doing it on my own that made me a leper. But they hadn't told anybody, or Gloria would have heard it. Mother would have heard it. Meg would have heard it. And you can believe that by sundown I would have heard it. By the same logic Meg hadn't known this morning, which now seemed a year ago. Or did she? She might have been going to tell me that when she left in a huff. That made me think of McLeod, whom I'd been carefully keeping out of my mind since I'd lammed out of his house. Bastard.

"How'd you know?" I asked Pete.

"Saw you go up a couple of times and followed you."

"Fink."

"You're the fink. What's the matter with school in New York?"

"Nothing. I just want out from home."

There was silence. I waited for him to say something about Gloria and his brother, half wishing he would and half wishing he wouldn't in case I would have to clonk him over the nose. But he didn't. I also wanted to ask him if Percy knew about McLeod, just to reassure myself. But that would have been a major blunder.

"Have a drag," Pete said, holding out his joint.

This is what I was afraid of. I'd gone along with the talk about finding pot because I didn't think there was a prayer of getting any. At school I was always in training for something or other—baseball, football, basketball, hockey—which was an acceptable excuse if you were a jock. The one time I'd smoked it with some of my class in the locker room, I had gotten so stoned they were scared to let me go home. Not that the faculty cracked the whip—most of them smoked grass themselves. But any cop who saw me would know exactly what I'd been doing, and in the state I was in

I'd probably tell him where and with whom. Actually, the whole thing scared me and I was glad to have the training excuse. I had a weird—but strong—feeling that pot was not for me, not because of the law or all the crap they hand out at school, tongue in cheek. And it didn't have anything to do with what anybody else did. It was just like there was some steering gear in me that kept pointing away from it.

But now I wasn't in training and Pete didn't know what had happened at school and I was tired of being out instead of in. I said as casually as I could. "I get sick on that stuff."

"Listen to the boy scout! You're just too good for us, Chuck. Maybe you'd better run back to teacher."

"He'll probably tell teacher, anyway, all about the nasty boys smoking grass."

"I told you, shove it! Here—" I took the joint out of Pete's hand. The mention of McLeod had done it. Gingerly, so I wouldn't show what an amateur I was, I took a drag, inhaling as little as I possibly could. Nothing happened. Then I took another.

"Here," Pete said. "Have one of your own."

In the beginning, it wasn't like the last time in the locker room, probably because I went at it cautiously. I lay back against a boulder. After a drag or two I started feeling relaxed. Then I felt good, like absolutely everything was going to turn out all right. And if it didn't, it still didn't matter.

"How'd McLeod get the scar?" Pete said.

Since everything had slowed down, it took me a a while to answer.

"In a car accident," I said dreamily. McLeod had really shoved me back. The memory of that morning sliced through my pleasant fog, bringing with it a muffled jab of pain and anger, so I added, "He was drunk and he had a kid with him who was burned to death."

"Wow! Hear that, you guys?"

The good feeling went. Something had gone wrong. I was afraid if I learned what it was everything would get worse, so I took another deep drag.

I can't explain what happened after that. Afterwards I figured I just passed out. Went to sleep. Had a nightmare, whatever. . . .

The sky and water seemed to swim together. Gulls were flying. After a while they seemed to be flying in formations and then I noticed they had jet engines and weren't gulls after all—they were planes. Then came a great, wonderful, floating feeling, because I was in one of the planes and sometimes I was in the sky and sometimes I was floating in the water only it was all the same. I got happier and happier. Then I landed on the water, just like one of the gulls, and got out of the plane and splashed through to the shore to my father who was standing there. I knew it was my father because the sun was blazing on his yellow hair. It was funny, though. I couldn't see his face because the sun was shining in it and it was just a blur. I said to my mother as I walked towards the shore, "But you must have another picture of him *somewhere*. How am I ever to know what he looked like?" And she said, "But that's why I threw the pictures away. I don't want you to know what he looked like, because then you might get to look like him and then you would hate me the way he did." Which is just the kind of thing you can expect from a female.

"But you were the one who hated *him*," I said. "That's why—"

I stopped because I suddenly realized I now could see Father's face very well. It had a red scar on one side, but it was getting smaller and smaller. It was odd, though, about his hair. I could have sworn it was yellow. I could see now it was black and gray. All of a sudden it was McLeod, minus scar. He was smiling and holding out his hands. I gave a shout and started running towards him. And that's where things went wrong, badly wrong. How, I don't know, but the sky was almost black. McLeod's face was as white as the stones and he was terribly angry. He was so angry I knew I would never be forgiven and that, anyway, I was going to die because I had forgotten about the undertow which was pulling me out and down, down into the water where I couldn't breathe. . . .

"Push his head down again," Pete said.

"No," I tried to say, as the water filled my mouth.

"Now you've drowned him." That was Sam.

There was a stinging slap on my face, then another. Slowly I came to. The sky wasn't black, it was its usual watery sun-and-blue effect.

"Come on, Chuck! Wake up! Do you want to get us all in trouble? If your mother sees you and squeals, we'll have the pigs all over this place."

I was standing, fully clothed, hip-deep in the water. The others, naked, were standing around. Pete gave me another slap. "Wake up!"

I tried to launch a blow that would knock his head off, but all I did was lose my footing and I had to be held up.

"I'm all right. Lemme go."

"Man! you weren't kidding, were you, when you said you got sick."

I pushed him away and staggered to the shore. I had barely gotten up onto the stony beach when I really got sick. Maybe it was the pot, maybe the sea water I had swallowed. Whatever it was, I felt like I was bringing up my breakfast of day before last.

I was shivering and my forehead was clammy with sweat, but, after a minute, I managed to crawl back to the water, wash my face and slosh some up on the beach to clean it up.

"You'd better stick to straightsville," Pete said, pulling on his pants. "You're a walking menace."

"Thanks a lot."

"You can go back in the rowboat," he went on grudgingly. "One of us can row the dinghy back."

"I can row it back myself."

"Suit yourself. I don't have to tell you that if you open your big mouth about this, we'll total you."

"Don't worry," I said sarcastically. "Your secret is safe with me." I swallowed the bad taste in my mouth. "What I told you about McLeod. Keep that to yourself, too."

"Who'd I tell?" Pete said, getting into the boat.

I tried to convince myself that since McLeod was a creep he deserved anything I did to him. But I couldn't make myself quit feeling lousy, like I had started something I couldn't stop. Shakily I got into the dinghy and, keeping the other boat well in sight, rowed back around the point.

For the first time in that putrid day, fate seemed to be for me. There was no one in when I got back to the house. I got out of my wet clothes, put on a dry pair of shorts and a sweater, laid the wet ones out on the garage roof outside my window where they could get the setting sun, and passed out on the bed.

The next morning early I sneaked down to get some milk and breakfast. I was starved. But even after I had eaten a couple of bowls of cereal and four pieces of toast with butter and honey and drunk two glasses of milk I didn't feel the way I usually do—rarin' to go. I felt like my head was stuffed with cotton and what I wanted to do was to go back to bed. I also didn't want to go up to McLeod's. As a matter of fact, it was the last place I wanted to go. I didn't know what to do.

I was sitting there, too zonked out even to move, when the door opened and Mother came in. What's more, she looked wide awake. If I hadn't been sitting down you could have knocked me over with one of Gloria's false eyelashes. Mother had on a silky blue robe that looked as if it had been made in Hong Kong or somewhere, and her dark hair was piled on top of her head and tied with a matching blue ribbon. She looked pretty enough to eat. If she had but known it, I was sitting there like ice cream on a dish for her to have. Luckily, I guess, she didn't know it.

"Where were you yesterday, Chuck?"

So that was the game. "With the gang."

"What were you doing?"

"What we always do. Swimming, shooting bull."

"Were you smoking marijuana?"

"No. Where would we get it around here?"

"Then why were you out like a light when we came in? Both Meg and I tried to get you up but you wouldn't stir. I'm worried about you, Chuck. Meg tells me you've found someplace to study. If that's what you were really doing, then all I can say is what I've been saying all along. You're studying too hard. You should be out with the others."

I pulled myself together. "First you grill me about what was I doing with the others, then you tell me I should be with them more." Against every inclination I stood up. "It doesn't matter what I do. It's wrong. Well, I'm going to pass that exam so I can go to St. Matthew's next year. That's why I'm studying."

"I don't want you to go to St. Matthew's. I don't want you to go to boarding school at all. You know what I think of them. I'm not sure whether I'll let you go even if you pass the exam."

It was funny. A couple of minutes ago I didn't think I ever wanted to see McLeod again and going up there to study seemed about as desirable as going to jail. The trouble with Mother was she didn't know when the odds were on her side. "I'm not going back to school in New York. If you don't let me go to St. Matthew's, then I'll drop out."

She looked frightened. "You can't—you can't drop out until you're sixteen."

"Then I'll leave home, and you can't stop me. Do you know how many kids my age are walking around the country? I'll go where you won't find me and don't think I don't have the contacts, because I do, any kid I know does."

Which was sheer bull, but Mother didn't know that. And given the way things are today, she couldn't be sure that I wouldn't get away with it.

At that moment the screen door opened and in walked Barry.

"Hi," he said. Then he did something that absolutely knocked me out. He went over and kissed Mother, right on the mouth, like he had every right to. Mother turned pink and her eyes looked bigger and browner than ever. It made me furious.

"Help yourself," I said nastily.

He turned around. Barry could lose twenty pounds, but I'll say this for him, he doesn't have a paunch and it's not flab. Square face, bluish eyes, light hair, what there is of it—Mr. Average, almost as pink as Mother, which didn't suit him the way it did her.

"Your mother has agreed to marry me, Chuck. I came by to tell you. I guess that was a tactless way of doing it."

He sounded apologetic, which turned me off. All I could think was that McLeod, if I had handed him lip like that, would have said something icily sarcastic that would have cut me down to size. Thinking about McLeod didn't make me feel any better, either, especially when I remembered that I had given him the bridegroom's role. For a second I tried to imagine him kissing Mother. I couldn't. It didn't work. I didn't know why it didn't, but it didn't.

"Congratulations," I said. "That's just what I need, another stepfather."

Barry looked at me, eyeball to eyeball. "Yes, Charles. That's what I think you need."

"Chuck!" Mother said. "Please be nice!"

I was about to say something else nasty when I remembered what we were talking about when Barry walked in.

"All right. Best wishes and all that. But I'm not going back to that school in New York."

"Is that St. Matthew's you want to go to?" Barry asked, going over to the stove and pouring himself some coffee.

"Yeah."

"It's not a bad school."

I'd been all braced for a fight and was therefore surprised.

"I thought it was supposed to be terrible," Mother said.

Barry took a swallow or two of coffee. "It went through a bad patch. It's okay now. And they've got a new headmaster who's beefing up the curriculum —Evans, I think his name is."

"That's the guy that wrote to me."

Gloria walked in. The two horizontal strips of knitted nothing she had on would not have filled a teacup. Other than that she looked like a free-floating thunderstorm.

"Aren't you afraid you're going to feel constricted in all those clothes?" Barry said.

"Gloria, go up and put on a shirt or something," Mother said. "You're practically naked."

"So what? It's my house." Gloria put some water in the kettle and put in on the stove. Then she got a bowl and poured herself some cereal.

"Please, Gloria."

"After I've had breakfast. Maybe."

Mother looked unhappy.

"Heard the news?" I said, curious as to whether

that was behind her scowl. "Mother's going to marry Barry."

"I heard it yesterday."

"Don't overdo the delight," Barry said amiably, "it might go to my head."

Gloria went on eating. Barry walked over and stood beside her. "Look, I'd like us to be friends. It makes it a lot easier for me, and, more important, for your mother. She'd like a little moral support."

"It's not as though it were the first time."

"In view of you and Chuck and Meg, that's on the whole rather a good thing, don't you think?"

Gloria didn't look at him. She swallowed another mouthful of cereal. "You've got Meg." That's our Gloria—if she's not first, she won't play.

"Yes, thank heaven," Barry said. "And here she is. Just like the Marines."

I don't know whether Meg had heard all that or not. She went over to Mother and gave her a smack on the cheek. Then she went to Barry. She not only gave him a smack. She put her arms around him. He bent and gave her a bear hug and lifted her off the floor.

"You'll get a hernia," Gloria said.

Mother looked at her quickly. "Gloria—that's mean!"

Barry put Meg down. "It would be well worth it. We'll go on a diet together after the wedding, Meg."

What I wanted to do was go back up to bed and sleep off this cottony feeling in my head. I don't mean my head hurt. But I felt funny, sort of unfocused. The house was obviously no place to sack out in today. Besides—more than ever I wanted to go to St. Matthew's now. And, for once, it looked like I might have some support.

I plunked my cereal bowl and the plate in the sink and headed for the door.

"Chuck, where are you going?"

"To study."

"Where—where do you study?"

There was a short silence, then I had an inspiration. "Up above the cove." The beauty about that was that it was true. McLeod's cliff was above the cove—by a couple of hundred feet. I just didn't add that it was also several miles further along the coastline.

"Well where do you keep your books?"

"There's an abandoned shack there." Also true. I could even shove a couple of old texts there for any snoop.

Barry was watching me. So was Gloria. I could feel my face beginning to get hot.

"S'long," I muttered, and started to leave.

"By the way, Chuck," Gloria said, getting up and pouring hot water into the drip pot, "that mangy animal of yours nearly bit Percy yesterday. You know if he ever bites anybody the vet'll have to put him away."

"And what was Percy doing to him?" I said angrily.

"Just trying to take a woodchuck away from him— like any humane person."

"Moxie has to hunt. Nobody feeds him around here. You have no right to interfere and you can tell your scrofulous boyfriend to keep his filthy hands away from him, or I'll—"

"You'll do what—lick him? He's on every team in his college. He'd make *mincemeat* of you, Chuck."

I was still boiling with fury when Barry said, "No one's going to hurt Moxie, Chuck. So keep your shirt on. She just said that to irritate you. When will you learn?"

Meg had got up and come to the door. "Come on, Chuck. Let's go."

As we walked down toward the road I finally said,

"All right. She laid the booby trap and I walked into it. But why does she do it?"

"Does it matter?" Meg said. "Besides. You know the answer. She has to be number one, like in the commercial."

"But why me?"

"Because you're handy. Because you let her get to you. Because she's jealous of you."

"Jealous of what, for the love of Mike? You mean from when we were babies?"

"Maybe. I wasn't around. You're good-looking and people like you. Gloria's good-looking, too, but people don't like her. She tries hard to make them, but after a while they all go away. You're the opposite. People would like to get closer to you but you won't let them. Were you smoking pot yesterday?"

The abrupt switch threw me off. "Is that any business of yours? I suppose now you're going to tell Barry." That was dirty and I knew it and was ashamed right away. But I felt so all-around lousy that I had to make somebody else miserable too.

Meg stopped dead in the road. "No, I won't tell Barry, though sometimes I think I ought to. If you're going to go and be a drug addict I don't think I'm doing you any good by not telling anybody. But I don't care as much as I used to, because you're not my friend any more. I guess you must be McLeod's friend. But I don't see why you can't be both. But you needn't bother now because I don't care any more."

"Megsy!"

"Let me go. I'm *glad* Barry is going to marry Mother. You just think I'm a nuisance now, but he *likes* me." She pulled her arm away and shot across the road towards the beach.

Joey once had his horoscope read and was really turned on because the swami or fortune-teller said Joey was going to have a great political career, except maybe he was also going to jail. But, as Joey said, today one often goes with the other, and maybe he should take up law as a preparation for politics.

I said law might also be useful if he got put in jail, and he agreed.

But what I'm getting at is I'd always looked on the whole horoscope scene as bull, but I was beginning to wonder if my moon or planet or whatever was in some undesirable place these past couple of days, because nothing was coming out right.

I was still sore at McLeod and I was thinking about this when I suddenly remembered the other thing that was bothering me: I had ratted on him.

I stopped walking. I had told Pete about McLeod's drunk driving and killing a kid. I now wished to God I hadn't. When I thought of what they could do with that—and how inevitably that would get the news to Mother about what I was doing all day—sweat broke out all over me. I'd done it because I was mad and, I suppose—I didn't like to think about this—to buy my way back into the good graces of Pete and the others. Talk about a fink!

I started walking again. The rest of the walk I tried to convince myself that in view of the way he'd acted towards me, I was justified. It didn't work too well. I still felt like a ratfink. If the whole family situation hadn't got worse instead of better, what with Barry joining the troops and adding one more body to our apartment, I might have turned back. But it had, so I went on.

CHAPTER 8

WHEN I WALKED into the library McLeod was standing by the fireplace staring down into what were probably last night's ashes. It sounds loony, but up here, even in early August, fires feel pretty good at night.

He looked up.

"Sorry to be late," I muttered, and slid into my seat at the table.

"I want to talk to you," McLeod said abruptly. For one sickening minute I wondered if he had already heard about my telling on him.

"Yes?" And added, without much conviction, "Sir."

But it wasn't what I was afraid of. It was somehow worse. Typically, he went straight to the point. "I'm sorry about—about what happened yesterday. I told you once that I had lived alone too long. I accused you of always running away. Well, that's what I did. Only instead of running I built a wall. Being a writer made it easy; easy to be up here earning a living, easy to be alone and keep clear of people."

Stubborn pride made me say, "It doesn't matter."

He looked at me then. "Doesn't it, Charles? Then why did you leave so abruptly?"

I had no answer to give. Or rather, I didn't want to answer, so we didn't say anything for a bit.

"Well?"

Nothing.

"If you can make me believe that I didn't make you angry, or hurt you, then I'll stop."

It was a hand held out, but I wouldn't let myself take it. How could I after ratting on him?

"Why can't we just forget it?"

"Is that what you want?"

"Yes."

"All right. Then let's get back to Vergil."

But it wasn't. As we crawled through the whole dreary Carthage bit, what I had told Pete was there like a ghost, getting larger and larger. Words that I knew perfectly well I couldn't remember. Whole parts that I knew we had gone through might as well have been new. Finally McLeod put down his book.

"What's the matter with you? You act as though you've never seen this. We went over it a few days ago."

That strange unfocused feeling was back. Pot doesn't affect any of the other kids this way—at least not that I knew of. But then I remembered hearing in school or reading in one of those dumb pamphlets they're always giving out that some people can't take it, like some people can't drink. This made me think about my father. Why, I don't know. Then I remembered the dream I had at the cove.

"Charles!"

McLeod's voice cracked like a whip. Suddenly he was standing over me. "What did you do yesterday?" he asked. "After you left here?"

Mother had asked that, but it wasn't the same. Besides, I had left her and come here. Now there was no more place to go to, and if there had been I wasn't at all sure I could get it all together and go there, or that I wanted to. . . .

"I went to the cove where my gang hangs out."

"And?"

"Smoked some grass." So now I had ratted on Pete and the others. But it didn't feel like ratting the way it had about telling on McLeod. I waited for him to wade in.

But he didn't. Not right away, anyway. Then he said wearily, "Oh, my God," and went and stood by the window.

"If your generation drinks, what's wrong with mine smoking grass. When you were in school didn't you ever sneak beer?"

"Yes."

"Then what's all the flak about?"

"How do you feel?"

"Fine. What's that got to do with it?"

"Because you're not concentrating very well—as you know."

"So? Did you ever have hangovers?"

"I thought marijuana wasn't supposed to give those."

"I'm not hung over. Look, Mc—Mr. McLeod. What I do when I'm not here is my own business."

The moment I said that I knew it was a mistake. This was the perfect opening for him to remind me that it was my idea being here, not his. I held my breath.

"That's true. But since trying to teach you when you're like this is like trying to get a bell tone out of cotton wadding, I'd appreciate it if you would desist while I'm coaching you. That is, if you want to pass that exam—and not waste my time and yours."

That sounded more like the old McLeod. But it was so much milder than I had expected that I felt almost let down. Besides, I had no intention anyway of smoking grass again.

He came over to the table and closed the book. "You might as well give yourself a holiday. You're not doing anything. Come back when you feel better."

I went back the next day. I still wasn't up to form, but I wasn't as zonked out as the day before. Another good night's sleep had helped a lot.

As the days passed I worked hard, harder than I had done before. After a while I realized that I was trying to get things back on the footing they'd been on before I'd made that stupid move in a burst of sympathy or something. It felt like a year since that morning, but it was only a week. I found myself thinking about it a lot, whenever I wasn't actually working. I still didn't understand it. I didn't understand McLeod. I didn't even understand me. But I saw what he meant about a wall, because he was back behind it.

In the background, I was vaguely aware that Mother and Barry were fluttering around on a kind of party circuit. Barry, who was now on vacation from his law firm, was nominally staying with some friends down the beach road, but every time I was at home he was there, amid such talk of wedding dates, apartment hunting, and what Gloria once acidly referred to as creeping *kitsch*. I tried a couple of times—but not very hard—to talk to Meg, but since she had left off visiting at her usual dawn hour and I was away from home during the day I didn't get much of a chance. What with my early rising, walking to and from McLeod's, and my six hours' work in between, I almost went to sleep with my head on the dinner table. Fortunately, Mother was too starry-eyed to ask any more leading questions about where I was going and what I was doing. Also, with Gloria the only holdout from the general rejoicing, they were concentrating on winning her over. They took her and Peerless Percy to anything they showed the faintest interest in going to— swinging parties, any summer stock in the area, a couple of music festivals with all-day picnics listening to Beethoven under the trees. Not so dumb, my sister Gloria. She was melting, but not rapidly enough so that their solicitude and desire to please should flag in any way. I could see their progress at dinner. Instead of the usual scowl, there'd be a soft smile and a side-long glance at Barry. Whether it fooled Barry or not, I somehow doubted. But it made Mother happy which, I grudgingly had to admit, was for him the all-important thing. I finally also decided that he wasn't as dumb as I had always thought, either. In his own way he was playing Gloria's game as cannily as she was, which in his case meant sitting there as stolidly as a tree stump while she whinnied and pranced and did the siren bit, so that she couldn't know she'd gotten anywhere—and (naturally) stop trying to please. But he'd pile on the outings, so she couldn't get sour through failing to score any goals.

When Gloria wasn't around, Barry's frozen front would thaw. Meg knew, I guess, what he was doing and why, because when Gloria wasn't around he'd kid and joke with her and she'd glow like a miniature sunflower. She was so happy, in fact, that she began eating less and looking less like a tub and more like the beginnings of a female. Not that I was up to noticing that much. But both Mother and Barry commented on it, and Meg lit up some more.

Nobody paid much attention to me. I think Barry had convinced Mother that my going to St. Matthew's was not a catastrophic idea. Because other than saying once, "I don't think you get enough exercise, Chuck," she let me alone.

Curiously, McLeod one day said the same. I was in sort of a limbo these days. After what had happened down at the cove I had no desire to go there. Just thinking about Pete made me feel guilty. On the other hand the kind of open-door relationship with McLeod that had kept me up there until after five in the past seemed gone. Sometimes I felt he had slammed the door. Other times that I had. I wasn't happy. I wanted to be friends with him, but every time I tried somehow to get through to him again I'd feel like Richard balking at a jump. I couldn't account for it because I had never felt this way before. I've always been a loner. Mother—and all five school analysts—have talked to me about that *ad nauseam*. Until now, I've felt it was a good thing. It kept me loose. Now all I could think about was that I had ratted on McLeod. It made me sicker than ever. All by itself it got to be a wall around me getting higher and higher. And the higher it got the less I could do about it, and, with a real show of logic, the sorer I got at McLeod.

Then one day as I was being particularly thick-headed he said, "I think you must need more exercise."

"I get enough."

"Doing what?"

"Climbing up here and down again, for one thing."

"For a boy—and an athletic one—of your age, who are you trying to kid?" He paused. "What about swimming?"

"It's too cold."

"I didn't know you were in such bad physical shape."

I could see by the clock on the chimney piece that it was eleven twenty. "Isn't it time for your ride?"

"That can wait."

He was looking at me and I was trying to read his expression. It certainly didn't show the warmth I had once seen. Sometimes I thought I would give almost anything to see it again, but the moment I thought that, a wave of sickening guilt came over me. Then I'd be like a stalled car.

"Well, this isn't getting us anywhere." He got up and left the room. Relieved, I waited to hear Richard's hooves. But in a few minutes McLeod was back carrying a knapsack in his hand.

"Come on."

"Where?"

"Never mind. Just come." The command was given in his usual autocratic fashion and was easier to obey than argue with. Besides, I didn't have much fight.

To my surprise he led me outside across the path to his car. "Get in."

"Where—?"

"Just get in."

It vaguely occurred to me that someone might see me with him. But that didn't seem important, either. When we got to the gate, instead of turning left onto the main road, he turned right into the cliff road that grew narrower and bumpier as it climbed. But the view from the top was really spectacular. I'd never seen it.

"Wow," I said. The sea was so blue it was almost green. There wasn't a house or a soul in sight. Just dark green rocky hills at left and in front, and to the right, the high edge of the cliff and the sea.

"Okay. Out you get."

I got out. "Where're we going?"

He came round the car. "We're going to play follow the leader. I lead. You follow."

"Aye, aye, sir," I muttered. What did he think I was—a Scout troop? But man, could he move!

We went straight for the cliff edge and then to my horror he stepped down into what looked like nothing. He turned, saw my face and laughed. "Don't worry. There's a path here."

There was: rocky, winding slowly down where, for a change, the cliff bulged out instead of in. Part of the path was where the rock naturally shelved out. Part looked as though it had been hammered out.

"How's your head for heights?" McLeod asked.

"Okay."

He started down. I followed.

I said, "You must be a climber."

"Yes."

"Where'd you climb?"

"Tetons, Rockies, Alps, Dolomites."

"What's the matter with Everest?"

"Too crowded."

A few minutes later we were down onto big, flat boulders. "Here." McLeod pulled some towels and trunks out of his knapsack. "Put these on."

They fit, but they looked ancient. "Where did these come from, the Ark?"

"I suppose you'd think so. They were mine, when I was about your age."

He had put his own on underneath his jeans, so all he did was step out of them and pull off his sweater. I guess he must have ridden Richard here a lot because he was tanned a lot darker than I. But all over one side of his body and down his leg were burns, some red, some paler, the skin shiny. Like his face, the other side was good—very thin, except for the hard muscles around his shoulders and arms and thighs.

"Dive in, Charles. It looks like an armchair but isn't. There's a current underneath. I'll go first." With that, he stepped to the edge of the rock and dived in. He came up about thirty feet away. "What are you waiting for?"

I went to the edge and headed in. It had been about two weeks since that day in the cove, and the water here, on the other side of the point, was colder. The shock almost paralyzed me. I came up by instinct more than anything else.

McLeod had swum back a little to where I was. "All right, now. Swim. Straight out."

I didn't hesitate—not with that cold. I plunged out. Feeling came back and suddenly I felt much better. Taking great mouthfuls of air I cut through the water.

I hadn't swum like that in a long time, because mostly at the cove and the pier and the beach we just fool around. I kept on going until I was ready to stop, McLeod about two yards to one side and keeping even. Then I started to play. I rolled over and duck-dived, then came up and rolled over some more and lay on my back, thrashing my feet, and then tried a backward dive. Coming up, I saw McLeod above me in the water and butted him gently in the stomach then shot away laughing as I came up. I felt marvelous. He turned, shaking the water out of his hair, and started after me. I knew I couldn't outswim him, so I went down again and swam underneath and looked around and there he was, so I surfaced and changed course and then went down and butted him again on the side.

I forgot he was an adult and a teacher and forty-seven years old. I even forgot what I had done to him. I forgot everything but the water and being in it and chasing and being chased, far from the shore with nothing around or moving except us. It was like flying. I thought suddenly, I'm free. And the thought was so great I poked him again on the way up. We swam some more, this time parallel with the shore, then played some more, then back to where we'd been.

"Okay. Let's go in," he said and turned towards the shore. I turned and we went together, although he took about one stroke to my three. If I hadn't seen how far one stroke carried him I would have thought he was just fooling around.

When I pulled onto the rock I realized that if I had been out any longer I would have been tired instead of just relaxed. The sun was hot and we lay on towels on a big flat rock above the one we used as a diving board.

The happy euphoric feeling should have gone on to a happy drowsy one, but even though I was physically

relaxed, it didn't. It was as though by stepping out of
the water I had lost that sense of freedom. It was too
bad, I thought, really too bad. But that terrible weight
was back.

And then McLeod, lying beside me, reached out
and with his hand grasped my arm, just the way I
had his two weeks ago.

"All right, Charles. Whatever it is, spill it. I'm not
just prying. But you can't carry it around much
longer. And I don't think I can watch any longer. It's
making you sick."

I thought of getting up and going, but his hand
was there, holding me. I could imagine it withdrawing
when he knew what I had done. I thought about the
water and the afternoon.

His hand tightened. "Come on, son."

Maybe it was the "son" that did it, although I'd
never liked it before when somebody said it.

"I ratted on you. I told Pete that day we were all
smoking grass how you got your scar, about being
drunk and the kid with you. It wasn't even that I was
stoned—I was later, a real bad trip, but not then. I
just wanted—I was sore at you. You made me feel
like I'd made some kind of pass at you. And they were
mad at me for studying and knew I came up here
because Pete saw me come. So he asked me how you
got the scar. So I told 'em. I'm sorry, McLeod. I feel
like an absolute skunk. A real fink."

What I wanted to do was cry like a baby. But I
couldn't do that, of course, so I put my other arm over
my eyes like the sun was getting into them. Curiously,
he hadn't withdrawn his hand. I waited to see if he
would in a delayed reaction, but he didn't.

"It's my fault as much as yours. I knew I had . . .
had hurt you, which was why I tried to talk to you
about it. I should have made you listen. Then you
wouldn't have been carting this load around."

But the load had rolled away. "Then we're still friends?"

"Yes, Charles. Still friends."

That great feeling I had in the water like, I guess, a sort of a high, came back. The sun was hot on my skin. The air smelled of salt and pines and grass (the real kind!) and hay. I felt super. I moved the arm he was holding and he let go instantly, but all I did was to slide my hand in his. I felt his fingers close around it.

After a while he said, "Tell me about that bad trip."

So I told him, and then about the dream. Until that moment I really hadn't thought much about it. But when I was finished I said, "I guess that means I wish you were my father."

"I wish so too."

"Did you ever have any sons?"

"No."

My mind drifted off. Then I said, "Meg asked me if I thought you'd be interested in marrying Mother."

There was a muffled laugh. "Your mother might not have cared for that arrangement."

"Maybe not. But when I think of The Hairball and Meg's father I'd think she'd be thrilled."

"Do you remember your own father?"

"A little." And then out of nowhere I said, "I have a funny feeling there was something wrong about him. Something the others know that I don't." I told him about the fracas at the beach three years ago with Gloria. "But I can't get anything out of anyone."

"Then don't try. And if some day you stumble over it, don't break your heart. We're all fallible. Like me. Like you."

I could imagine what all the kids I knew, even Joey, would say about the way I felt about McLeod. But here, lying beside him on the rock, I didn't care.

I didn't care about anything. Everything else, everybody else, seemed far away, unimportant.

"I like you a lot," I said.

There was something beating in his hand or mine, I couldn't tell which. I wanted to touch him. Moving the arm that had been across my eyes I reached over and touched his side. The hot skin was tight over his ribs. I knew then that I'd never been close to anyone in my life, not like that. And I wanted to get closer.

But at that moment McLeod sat up and then stood up. He stood facing away from me for a minute. Then he jumped down onto the lower rock. In a minute he was back, dressed. He smiled down at me. "Up. You may not feel like it, but if you stay here longer you'll get cold."

"That's a lot of bull."

"Maybe. Have you forgotten you have three hours of study yet? To say nothing of eating something?"

"Couldn't we take the day off?" I asked, as winningly as I could.

"Certainly not. Get dressed. The trip back up the cliff should wake you up. I'm going ahead of you. It's easier up than down."

As the car bumped over the path, and McLeod swerved to avoid the worst potholes, muttering under his breath when we hit one, something that had been bothering me suddenly made me say, "McLeod—"

"Yes? You can call me Justin, by the way."

I was pleased. "All right."

"What were you going to ask?"

I blurted out, "Do you think I'm a queer?"

"No, I do not think you're a queer." He glanced down at me. "Because of this afternoon?"

"Yes."

"No. Everybody wants and needs affection and you don't get much. Also you're a boy who badly needs a father."

That was what Barry had said. But I didn't tell him about Barry and Mother. I didn't want to think about home at all. I felt like I was in a sort of golden cocoon and I didn't want to break out of it.

CHAPTER 9

I LIVED IN THAT GOLDEN COCOON for a month. Of course I didn't know it was only going to be a month, or maybe I did. But whenever the thought that it might end came, I pushed it away, and little by little I came to believe it would last forever.

I forgot everything else—the family, the gang, the cove, New York, even St. Matthew's and the coming exam which was the reason I was there in the first place. And the fates that had conspired to louse everything up for me in the past, now changed their minds and made everything easy.

For one thing, for large parts of the time the family wasn't even there. Mother and Barry spent the rest of his vacation in New York looking for a new apartment. Gloria's father came back from his think tank on the coast and invited her to go with him and his wife to Mexico for a couple of weeks. Gloria was not as ecstatic as you would suppose. For one thing, there was the impending arrival of Sue Robinson, who might well use the time to re-annex Peerless Percy. For another, Gloria's father, in a switch of taste, had married a tweedy English lady with all the correct intellectual viewpoints but a bad habit of reverting to outmoded discipline in such matters as doing one's own thing—especially, Gloria complained, if it were her thing. But Mexico is Mexico. So Gloria went. With all of them gone, Meg left for a camp further down the coast for a couple of weeks, and I was officially boarded with the Lansings, which was no sweat for me, since they had been successfully brought up by their children never to ask where I'd been or intended to go.

Actually, most nights I spent at home on account of Moxie, which was great. He had the run of the house, various parts of which started smelling the way he does. I suppose I counted on Mother's being too bride-minded to care. I don't know what I thought. A sort of happy idiocy seemed to take hold of me.

McLeod said to me one day when I was in the water horsing around, "I don't know whether to be flattered or frustrated at the change in you."

"What change?"

"You're getting younger by the hour."

"Isn't that supposed to be a good thing?"

He grinned. "If you're fourteen to begin with it doesn't leave much room for backing."

We swam almost every day, because along with the other goodies was a spell of gorgeous weather.

"I feel free," I said, lying on my back and paddling my feet.

"Which is what you always wanted to be. Did it ever occur to you that the word 'free' doesn't mean anything by itself?"

"How so?"

"Free to do what? Free from what?"

One of the answers was easy and I had already answered it: free to do what I wanted. The other required some thought. In that water you don't laze about too long. I took some slow-motion strokes thinking about it. Freedom from what?

From being crowded.

From Mother.

From Gloria.

From home.

I told this to McLeod.

"I know they get in your hair. You probably get in theirs just as much. But don't you love them at all?"

That word. "I don't like the word 'love,'" I said.

"It's become debased, overused. It's still a good word. Why do you dislike it?"

I stopped swimming and trod water. The shore seemed far away, a wavy green line between two blues. "I don't know. It's always turned me off, as far back as I can remember." I tried to push my memory back. All I got was darkness. But the darkness was full of an uncomfortable feeling. "Something," I said. "I can't exactly remember."

"But it's linked to your dislike of the word 'love'?"

I started to nod. My head went under a little and I swallowed some water. Then I felt it, a much colder stream seemed to grab my feet and pull. It frightened the daylights out of me. I couldn't get to the surface. I kicked out as hard as I could and made it. When I got up I thought I must have blacked out for a minute and been swept out miles from the shore because it was nowhere in sight. The fear turned into an iron ball inside me. The cold from the current seemed to shoot up through me. Then I must have turned, because there was the shore. But I was right about one thing. I was further out.

"Justin," I cried.

"Right here." He was behind me. "Come on, Charles, let's go in, slow and easy."

"Im being pulled."

"That's the undertow. If you start swimming now you'll be all right. It doesn't reach the surface, so level out. Swim."

His voice broke my panic enough to make me try

to do what he said. But it wasn't enough. "I can't. It's pulling me."

"You can. Now do as I tell you. At once!"

There was that authoritarian lash that always made me furious. Fascist, I thought, kicking savagely. Wait till I get back.

We were about halfway to the shore before I realized the icy undertow was no longer pulling at my feet. By comparison the water felt warm.

"Want some help?" McLeod said. He was less than a yard from me.

"You can keep your help," I muttered, and swallowed some water.

"Good thing there's no sewage this way."

That happy comment almost brought the water up. I coughed and spat and gave him a dirty look.

"You and your delicate stomach," he said amiably, rolling over like a porpoise. I was tired but I gathered myself and ducked under. Just as I was about to butt him where it could knock the wind out of him, I felt my hair grasped. The next thing, I was being hauled up like a bunch of seaweed.

"Gently, Tiger, gently. Mustn't butt teacher."

I tried to get at him, flailing my arms. But his arm was too long.

"Tut!" Then he let go my hair and was off. It wasn't far to the shore, but I saw how he could really move. There was a streaking flash through the water and then he had pulled himself up on the diving rock and was watching me.

Feeling about as agile as a barge, I lumbered up. At what I thought would be just about my last stroke I reached the rock and crawled up. All I wanted to do was lie down.

He threw my towel at me. "Take off your wet trunks and rub hard."

"Later."

"Now."

"For Chris'sake," I moaned. "Do I have to do everything your way?"

"At the moment, yes. I want you to be dry this time before you lie down."

I pulled off my trunks and rubbed the towel sideways and diagonally and across my back. I rubbed my chest and stomach and legs. Then I climbed up onto the flat rock and lay down.

"And I don't like profanity," Justin said from somewhere below me.

"So solly, sir," I said, and the next moment was asleep.

I awoke when cold. water splashed on my face.

"All right, Endymion, let's move."

McLeod was standing over me in his jeans, but no sweater which, in a minute, I realized was over me, along with his towel. He was pouring water over my face from a rusted can.

I sat up on my elbows. "What time is it?" We had come out at noon and the sky didn't look like it was anywhere near noon.

"About three."

I gave a huge yawn and got up.

We bumped back most of the way in silence. I was remembering what had happened, rather ashamed both of my panic and my bad temper. I wondered if he thought I was chicken.

With that kind of ESP he had, he said, "I shouldn't have let you go out so far. I was listening to what you said and wasn't paying attention. I'm sorry."

I was beginning to put things together. "Is that why you started giving orders like a Nazi SS colonel?"

"It was the fastest way to get some adrenalin going in you. I could have towed you in. But I thought you'd like it better if you made it on your own."

"Do you think I'm chicken?"

"Feeling afraid isn't chicken."

"But acting like it is."

"You want instant heroism?"

"You mean it takes practice?"

"Yes. Like everything else."

"Like you," I said.

He said sharply, "I'm not a hero, Charles. Don't make me one."

"Why not? I think you are."

"Because." He veered the car around a large hole and looked down at me. "One day you'll find I have clay feet—and knees and legs. If you've built me up as a hero you'll never forgive me for breaking that image. Do you understand?"

I didn't, really. I was holding the golden cocoon together. I shook my head.

"Then take my word for it." He started the car up again and we bumped down to his gate.

I decided he was just underrating himself and to forget about it.

The next day I remembered what we had been talking about when I hit the undertow. I tried to explain to Justin about the sense of darkness and discomfort when I tried to remember too far back. We had finished the coaching early and I was drinking some milk and eating some cheese and fruit and locally made bread that Justin said was better for me than a pound or so of cookies. I cut a large hunk of cheese and put it on a piece of bread.

He grunted. "Well, I am neither a detective nor a psychiatrist and I'm not sure self-probing—except when necessary and when you know what you're doing —doesn't make things worse rather than better. Some things you just have to accept."

I took a large bite. "I thought knowing yourself was supposed to be a big deal," I said around it. It didn't come out too clearly.

"Try that again after you've swallowed—and before you take the next bite."

I swallowed. "A teacher at my school said that manners are an elitist device for preserving status by giving the proletariat a sense of inferiority."

"I think it's worth risking. Don't talk with your mouth full."

I remembered Peerless Percy and all the wet doughnut around his teeth. "Okay."

"What was it you said before?"

"I thought knowing yourself was supposed to be the big deal."

"Self-knowledge is one thing, self-preoccupation another. Do you still want to go in the Air Force?"

"Yes," I said, and realized I hadn't thought about flying for a couple of weeks. "But I haven't thought about it lately. Why—don't you like the idea?"

"If that's what you really want, it's fine. But not if it's an escape fantasy."

"How will I know whether it is or not?"

"Is space—being an astronaut—any part of your ambition?"

It was something I had never said to anyone, astronauts, as part of the military-industrial establishment, not being very highly thought of at my school. "Well . . . yes."

"Then you'll know how real your ambition is when you come to the mathematics you'll have to know to be one. It takes work—not daydreaming."

"Meg said mathwise I was still with the Wright brothers."

"That's the sister you like?"

"Yes, Meg's okay."

"She's also right about your math. You're going to have to buckle down, Winsocki, buckle down."

"What's that—a poem?"

"An old song, long before your time."

"Do you think I can do it—be an astronaut? They're very bright."

"You're bright as you need to be. All this talk about your being stupid is so much smoke screen. It's a combination of self-pity and cop out. It lets you off having to work at things you don't want to do."

"Thanks a lot."

He smiled—he had a really great smile. "Don't mention it."

I wasn't mad. I didn't really think any more that I could be mad at him, not the way I was when I slammed out to the cove that day. Except for Joey I'd never had a friend, and he was my friend; I'd never really, except for a shadowy memory, had a father, and he was my father; I'd never known an adult I could communicate with or trust, and I communicated with him all the time, whether I was actually talking to him or not. And I trusted him. Which doesn't mean to say that he ever let me get away with anything, and he didn't like excuses as to why I didn't do something right.

"It's too bad you can't relate to spelling," he said sarcastically one day. "And if you're opening your mouth to tell me that spelling is a racist plot, don't. Here's a list of words I want you to learn. I'm tired of seeing them misspelled. I'll test you on them tomorrow. And they'd better be right."

"You've got to be kidding. That's mid-Victorian."

"You're free to go."

"Your way or no way."

"Correct."

So I learned the words.

It went on like that.

Most days we swam. On the occasional gray day we walked, carrying sandwiches, drinking out of the streams. Back of the peninsula was some wild country, too rocky for farming, with sometimes the shell of a house or mill. Further up the coast the spruce and fir and pine came down to the water's edge and walking through them was like being in silence the way you are in water when you're swimming.

"It's spooky," I said once.

"That's because you're not used to silence. There's nearly always something making a noise: radio, television, phonograph, traffic, voices."

"Is that why you live up here alone?"

"Partly. And being used to it now, I find the racket that most people live with unbearable."

"Why did you come here to live?"

He hesitated. "I lost the job I had under circumstances that made it unlikely I'd get another one."

"Did it have something to do with your accident?"

"Yes."

I'd wondered about that crash, but after feeling so ratty about telling Pete, I didn't want to press it further. I suppose I wanted, in some way, to show Justin that as far as I was concerned it didn't matter.

He said abruptly, "I was in prison for two years after that."

The words came out of that great pool of silence among the trees. I wasn't really surprised. I'd never known anyone who'd been in prison although there was always a lot of talk about how terrible things were there and making them better now. Suddenly, prison was not just something on TV news. It was a real place where Justin McLeod, my friend, had spent two years.

"Was it awful?"

"In some ways. But I was lucky. It was one of the better prisons. Also I had fully expected to go. I had pled guilty and thought I would get a longer sentence. I learned a lot there."

"What kind of thing?"

"About myself, and other people. Also I started writing there. When I got out I knew I couldn't go back to what I'd been doing, and I wanted to be alone."

I remembered his name and the words *St. Matthew's School* at the beginning of the poetry anthology.

"Did you teach at St. Matthew's?"

"Yes."

There wasn't anything left to say. But I wanted him to know that it didn't make any difference to me.

"It doesn't matter, you know. I mean. . . . You know what I mean."

He looked down at me and smiled. "Yes, I know. Thanks."

In a way that conversation made the coaching part easier. He knew how things were taught and what I could expect on the exam.

"Barry said St. Matthew's is better than it used to be. That it had gone through a bad patch but Evans, the new guy, is good."

"He is."

I was really enjoying lessons, even math and Latin. I was enjoying everything. One day I said, "We'll always be friends, won't we?"

I was standing on a rock at the top of a hill, the highest point in that area. Jusin was standing a little below. He said,

"As long as you want us to be."

"That'll be always."

He smiled. "All right."

I felt a worry. "I won't change." Then, as he didn't say anything, "Why should I change?"

"Today is enough. You can't lock up tomorrow and keep it safe."

"How do you mean?"

"It doesn't matter. I think it's going to rain. Let's go."

CHAPTER 10

AND THEN ONE DAY it was over.

It all happened because I forgot it was Sunday.
Saturdays had long since been absorbed into the rest
of the week. I spent them with Justin, not working,
but swimming, walking, reading, arguing, even letting Richard get used to me, so that by the end of
August I could not only pet him, I had even ridden
him once or twice. But Sundays I spent down on the
community beach or on the jetty—waiting for the
day to pass.

This time, maybe because Justin didn't remind me
on Saturday with his usual "I'll see you Monday,"
I forgot. So I arrived at about seven thirty, walked
into the house, saw Justin wasn't in the library, and
went through to the kitchen. He was there, drinking
coffee with a book propped on a wire stand in front
of him. What stopped me was that he had on a white
shirt and tie and a tweed jacket. I had never seen
him in anything but work pants or jeans and a
sweater or sweat shirt.

"Why are you dressed up?" I asked, without saying good morning or anything.

"It's Sunday. Or didn't you remember? You're supposed to have the day off."

"Oh." I felt let down.

"Want some milk?"

"Yes, thanks. I'll get it."

"I don't want to seem inhospitable," he said as I brought the milk back to the table, "but I'm going to have to leave you in a few minutes."

"Where are you going?" Not that it was any of my business. I guess I didn't expect him to answer. But he did, and really surprised me.

"Church. You're spilling the milk."

I was. It was overflowing the glass. I yanked a towel off the back of a chair. "Why are you going to church?" I asked, mopping up the overflow.

"No, don't hang it up again. Put it in the sink. For the usual reason—to participate in public worship."

"Oh."

"Haven't you ever been to church?"

I shook my head. "No."

Justin swallowed the last of his coffee and got up. "I'll be back in a couple of hours."

I heard him go through into the hall and then out the front door. He was almost at his car when I caught up with him. "Can I go with you?"

He hesitated. "What would your mother say?"

"Mother believes in people making their own choices," I said piously. I didn't add—except when she doesn't approve of the choices, like boarding school.

But Justin knew, too, or guessed. "You're not a good liar, Charles."

"Well, she did say that when people reach the . . . the age of discretion, they should do what they think is right."

"I doubt if she'd think fourteen is the age of discretion, but you look holy enough for wings when you say that. Do you realize also that somebody might see you with me? You're very secretive about your coming up here and it might be somebody who would tell your family—not just a friend."

"Nobody my family knows would be up at this hour on Sunday morning."

He laughed. "All right. But you may—probably will—be bored."

But I was scrambling in. "Do I look okay? I mean—I'm not dressed up or anything."

"If you looked a little worse it might be better—might make them feel you had been snatched from the fires just in time." He started the car.

"Shall I get out and roll in the dirt?"

"No use overdoing it."

Mickey's big head came in the window. Justin gave him a pat and a push. "No, Mickey."

"Don't you think he needs church?"

"It's more whether church needs him. He likes to join in. When it comes time to sing or chant he howls."

"Maybe he doesn't have a musical ear."

"My own view is the opposite: he does. That's his problem."

By this time the front third of Mickey was in.

"Oh, all right," Justin said. He gave a big push, then leaned back and opened the back door. "You're having a bad influence on him, you know. He used to be resigned to staying home."

With Mickey occupying all of the back seat we started off. "What kind of dog is he?" I asked, as Mickey's tongue wetly and affectionately enveloped one ear.

"Who knows?"

"I mean, you didn't buy him as some special breed?"

"I didn't buy him at all."

"How did you get him, then?"

"I found him, on the side of a road. He'd been either thrown out of a car or maybe run over by one. His back legs were broken."

"How old was he?"

"The vet said around three months."

"How could anybody do that?"

"I don't know."

It was a nice ride, away from the main highways, through rolling green fields crisscrossed by stone walls. The farther in we got the bigger the trees looked.

"Where are we going?"

"Merton."

Half an hour later we turned into Merton, with its two main streets cutting across one another and converging on a tiny green. Justin drew up at a white frame church and parked. Leaving a window open so Mickey could get out if nature called, we got out.

Justin looked at Mickey. "Stay!" he said firmly.

"Do you think he will?" I asked as we went in.

"We'll see."

Despite what Justin said I wasn't bored, although I had no idea what was going on. But I got up and sat down when he did and, feeling a little foolish, knelt. He paid no attention to me. The man up at the front running the proceedings seemed about a hundred and two. He had on a red tunic thing over a white robe and spoke in a tiny wispy voice. Despite that, or maybe because the church had the right acoustics (The Hairball was great on acoustics and explained them to me), I heard most things he said. I tried to make some sense of it. But instead of getting clearer it got foggier. Maybe there wasn't enough air in the church, although some of the colored glass windows were tilted open and it was quite cool. I felt strange. The church wasn't exactly light, but it wasn't dark, sort of a dusk. There was a huge crucifix off at one side, in an alcove. There were candles there and other places. They seemed to blur. There was a funny, not unpleasant, and oddly familiar smell. I couldn't hear the old man any more, though

I knew he was still talking. Then there was a blackness and I felt both afraid and angry, but I couldn't tell which. I blinked a few times and tried to get focus back. But it got worse, not better. I looked over towards Justin, and panic hit me. *I couldn't see his head.* I know it sounds crazy. And I was sure then I must have freaked out. But although I could see his body including his shoulders and I knew his head was there, I couldn't really see it. Maybe it was just the light or something. But it just blurred into everything else.

"Justin," I said. Then dizziness hit me, and I knew I had to get out. I turned and made for the door as fast as I could.

When I was outside I sat on the low wall running around the churchyard and waited for everything to settle. Almost right away I felt better. In a couple of minutes Justin came out.

"Are you all right?"

I nodded. "I'm sorry, Justin."

"Nothing to be sorry for. Do you think you can make it to the parish house? It's only a few feet."

The panicky feeling started again. "I don't want to go inside."

"All right. But I'll go in and get some cold water. It might make you feel better."

I shook my head. "I don't need it, thanks. Truly, I'll be fine." I remembered then about not being able to see his head and looked up. He looked the same as he always did, except that I noticed, for the first time in a long while, that half his face was scarred. I know I must have blown my mind, because I reached up and put my hand on his face. "It's your face," I said.

"Yes. Whose did you think it would be?"

The words came from nowhere. "My father's."

We stared at each other. Then I pulled my hand away. "Justin, can we go? I want to get away from here."

"Yes. Of course."

I didn't feel too much like talking, so we just rode along. I tried to figure out what had happened to me, but every time I thought about it I started getting upset again, so I didn't think about anything.

When we got back to his house I said, "I suppose I ought to go down to the village beach for the rest of the day. Today being Sunday, I mean."

"Do you want to go?"

"No."

"Then don't."

When we were back in the kitchen he said, "Sit down." I did. He filled two bowls with something from a large pot on the stove and brought them to the table. "Start," he said putting down a big spoon. Then he brought a dark loaf on a board, cut two slices, handed me one, and sat down.

The soup was hot and very good, thick, with meat and vegetables and something that looked—but didn't taste— like rice. "Is this rice?" I asked.

"No, barley."

"Did you make it? The soup?"

"Yes."

"Do you like cooking?"

"Not particularly. But I don't have much choice." I thought of Barry. "You could have a housekeeper."

"I prefer to cook."

"This is good," I said, cleaning up the bowl.

"Want some more?"

"Yes. What's in it?"

He got up and went to the stove. "Everything." He came back and put the refilled bowl in front of me. "But you start with a beef bone. If Mickey has been chewing on it a week or so it's even better. More flavor."

I was on the point of swallowing a spoonful. "You're kidding."

"What makes you say that?"

"Funny man. You crack me up."

He smiled.

After I was through, Justin said, "You can go upstairs and lie down if you want to. Might do you good
to sleep."

"I'd rather lie on the rock. Could we?"

"Sure."

So we drove down. I lay on the rock in the sun and
went to sleep. When I woke up we swam. We got
back onto the rock a while later and lay there. All
this time Justin hadn't said anything about what happened. I sort of knew he wouldn't. I lay there and
thought about that. If it were Mother or The Hairball or Meg's father or any of the teachers at school
or even Meg, they'd be all over me. What happened?
Why? Tell me all about it. Are you sure you feel all
right. . . .

"Justin," I said.

"Yes."

"You're a great guy. I mean you really are."

"Thanks. Why?"

"Because you're not all over me asking a bunch of
questions."

"I've asked you some from time to time."

"Not when I didn't want to answer them. How do
you always know the difference?"

"I suppose because I—"

I turned over on my side, facing him. "Because you
what?"

"Luck, I guess."

"It's not luck. You weren't going to say that."

"Because we're friends."

"Yes. We are." I was getting drowsy again. "I have
a feeling that if I don't think about it, it'll suddenly come to me, why I got dizzy, I mean."

"Probably."

"Why do you think it happened?"

"Charles—how do I know?" His face turned a little and he looked at me. "You said you'd never been to church. It looks like you had and something happened there that upset you a lot only you don't remember it. Maybe you deliberately blocked it out."

It was true. I knew it, though I still couldn't remember what it was. The sun was hot. I was still on my side, one arm under my head. Just as I was dropping off I put the other across his chest, feeling the skin and hair under my hand. A sort of an electric feeling went through me. I half sat up.

"Justin."

"Go to sleep, Charles," he said firmly. "And let me do the same."

It seemed like a good idea, so I lay back down again and went to sleep.

When I woke up I was in the same position, one arm under me, one across Justin's chest. I yawned and tried to move. "My arm's asleep."

"Rub it," he said unsympathetically. "I'm going in."

After another swim we came back to the house. It was around four o'clock. Justin went out to see Richard. I went into the library and immersed myself in one of his Terence Blake books. I had long since swallowed whole the ones I hadn't read. I was now rereading the lot. I only became aware of the passage of time when Justin switched on the lamp beside me.

"Thanks," I muttered, and plunged back in.

A while later he came to the door. "Come on, Charles. Dinner's ready." I looked up. It was almost dark.

Dinner was more of the same: soup, bread, cheese, a large salad, cold meat and fruit. By the time we were finished it was dark. I washed the dishes as a gesture towards not having done anything about dinner. When I was through he said, "I'll drive you down to your house."

"Can't I stay here tonight, Justin?" When I said it I knew that was what I had been planning to do all along.

"No. I think you'd better go on down. What if the Lansings suddenly remember their responsibilities and wonder where you are?"

"They won't. Besides, I spend most of the nights at home anyway because of Moxie."

"All right, what about Moxie? Who's going to feed him?"

Of course it was true that Moxie fed himself most of the year, but that was when the house had been shut up and he knew I'd gone. I hesitated. I don't know whether I was still shook up or not, but I didn't want to be alone. Or, more specifically, I didn't want to be away from here.

Justin was watching me. "Let's get one thing straight. I'd like to have you here. Any time and for as long as you wanted. But I think we'd better not push your luck."

He was right, of course, although I didn't like to be reminded of life outside the golden cocoon.

"Okay."

He dropped me off near the Lansings'. I went in. Nobody was there, which was more or less what I expected. The Lansings, with Pete away and Barney now at camp, did a lot of partying. I left a note saying I was going down to my house and went back out again and walked down along the shore to our cottage.

CHAPTER 11

THE DOWNSTAIRS LIGHT WAS ON. It always is, so I didn't think anything about it.

"Moxie," I yelled.

Usually there's a gravelly meow and Moxie emerges from somewhere, or I hear him softly padding down the stairs.

But there wasn't a sound. "Moxie, come on, boy. Dinnertime." I moved towards the kitchen, and then I heard him. The stairs come down near the kitchen and he was lying at the bottom. It was a kind of low cry. He was lying on his side. There was blood around his mouth. He was trying to get up, but his back legs wouldn't move.

"Oh, God, Moxie. What happened to you?" I bent down and tried to move him, which was dumb, dumb, dumb. But I wasn't thinking. He gave a cry. More blood oozed out. I stroked his head and then went to the phone. I tried the only vet in the area that I knew of. There was no answer and no answering service although I dialed it three times and let it ring. Then I got the operator and she tried a couple on the other side of the county. One was away on vacation and his office was closed. His stand-in was away for the weekend. She tried another. He was on duty and couldn't leave. He told me to try and get Moxie there in a car and gave me instructions as to how I should lift him. I called Justin. But there was no answer. I didn't know what to do.

I stood there, wondering which of the neighbors to call first, which one had a car here. The thing about our summer community is that you don't need a car once you're here. That's supposed to be the beauty of it. Men bring their families here, leave them, and drive back. Often they take their own vacations out in long weekends, but by Sunday night most of them have gone. I tried one or two. Either they weren't home or didn't have a car. I rang the Lansings, in case they had returned. But there was no reply. I tried to make my mind work efficiently, but I was watching Moxie who was obviously dying. I tried a couple more places. The Brandons didn't have a car and Maurice had already left. The Goulds didn't answer. I dialed Justin again. No answer. I knew, because he told me, that he often took walks at night.

Of course the local directory was no good. People are only here for the summer and their names aren't listed. I never used the telephone so I couldn't figure how Mother knew to call people until I remembered that she has a personal book—a blue one—in which she wrote down all the numbers she needed. I opened the drawer under the telephone and threw all the directories on the floor. There was the local one, one for Manhattan, one for Westchester, one for Connecticut, one for Boston. The yellow pages. But no little blue book. I decided it would probably be in her room—or Gloria's. Gloria was forever on the phone.

I took the stairs two and three at a time and went first into Mother's room. Turning on the light I zipped through everything that was visible, blessing her, for once, for her neatness. Meg's room came next.

I switched on the light and gave a quick look. Meg is not neat. As I looked through her books and magazines I flung them onto the floor and then went through her drawers. No book. I knew I didn't have it so I went back past Mother's room to Gloria's.

The moment I opened the door I knew that Moxie had been in here and done something bad. I switched on the light. Right in the middle of the bed he had given his all. The blue book was there all right, on Gloria's dresser.

I took it and was headed for the stairs when I heard sounds. There was a voice talking and then a loud metallic squeak. It could only come from my room and my bed. I veered off, thrust open the door and switched on the light.

Peerless Percy and Gloria were there. And I didn't need any advanced class in sex education to know what they were doing.

Gloria gave a gasp. "Get out," she shrieked.

Percy turned. "Cripes!" He made a snatch at his pants.

But I wasn't looking at either him or Gloria. I was staring at his tan Mexican boot on the floor right in front of me. There was blood drying on it and in the blood were stuck some ginger hairs.

Rage exploded in me. "You—you! . . ." The words jammed in my throat. Then I got my voice. "You kicked Moxie. You've nearly killed him! Did you know that, you creep—you lousy stinking slob?" A fury I had never known possessed me.

Percy is four years older than I am and on his freshman hockey team. There was a baseball bat in the corner. I picked it up and waded in.

I don't remember too much of what immediately followed. Gloria shrieked again and kept on shrieking. I kept trying to land one on Percy and succeeded in whacking him on the shoulder a couple of times. At first he kept saying he didn't mean to hurt Moxie, but I wasn't listening. Then he got mad. He won, of course. He could hold my arm long enough to keep me from braining him, and with some judicious biting Gloria managed to get the bat from my hand. I still fought and got in a couple of kicks, but he finally socked me and I fell against the bed's headboard.

"Listen, kid," he said, feeling the arm where I had left a welt. "Just thank your stars I don't really teach you a lesson. You freaking brat. You deserve one."

I was panting and trying hard not to cry. "You jerk! You killed my cat. That's all you're good for, kicking helpless animals."

Gloria had run out. Percy was struggling into his boots.

"It's your fault letting him mess up the house. The place stinks."

My head was aching where it had cracked against the headboard. Also that blind, blazing rage had receded. What was I doing here, with Moxie downstairs? I sprang up. Percy pushed me back on the bed. "Not so fast," he said, straightening his shirt. "You'll go when I say."

"Moxie's down there. I've got to get him to a vet. Let me by."

I shot past him and down the stairs. Moxie was still alive, but only just. I knew there was no use. His eyes were beginning to glaze. All I could do was wait it out with him. I sat on the floor beside him, stroking him and talking to him.

Percy came down and past without saying anything. When he got to the door he turned.

"I'm sorry about Moxie," he said. "I only used my boot when he went for Gloria with his teeth and claws. He's your cat, man. You let him take over the place. It was my boot, but you did it as much as me."

I didn't say anything.

Moxie died about an hour later. Percy was telling the truth. It was his boot. But it was as much my fault as his. I sat there on the floor for a long while. Then I got an old laundry bag from the hall closet, put Moxie in it and took him out behind the garden up the hill. There was a bright moon, but I slipped a flashlight in my pocket anyway. I also took a shovel from the basement.

I dug a grave up the hill under the big sycamore tree, so I would always know where Moxie was buried. It took much longer than I had thought it would, although I didn't care. But the soil is rocky and it had been a dry summer. Then I came back to the house and cleaned up the mess on the floor.

Then I went upstairs.

When I got to my room my bed had been smoothed. In the middle of the blue spread were some sheets of paper clipped together, with a note in Gloria's handwriting:

I've been saving these for you.

They were duplicated news clippings. And they they told me everything I had always wanted to know about my father.

I stood there, reading. Some of it, of course, I knew: graduate engineer M.I.T., Navy pilot Korean War, the Distinguished Flying Cross and the Navy Cross, both of which I had in New York.

What I didn't know was that he had died of chronic alcoholism in Sydney, Australia, where he had been living on skid row for some years.

I suppose I could have called Justin, but I wasn't thinking very clearly. For one thing, the minute I read the news clipping I remembered, mostly, what had happened in church that evening long ago. I had gone with my father. Then I had gone to sleep. When I woke up two men were hauling him out. They hadn't seen me. I remembered his head, sagging between them. I remembered that it was cold, the bunches of candles making one blurred light, and I remembered running down the church aisle after the men, screaming at them. It was dark when I got outside and found Father sprawled on the pavement.

Tonight, Moxie, this morning, that evening—all went together, like one of the new flicks. It made sense of Father, Mother, and me. Mostly me.

I put on a pea jacket, stuffed the papers in my pocket, and put the flashlight in the other. Then I left the house and started on the long climb up to Justin's.

I didn't think on the way up there. Pictures slid in and out of my mind in no particular order: the church this morning with Justin, Father's blond head in the sun with me on his shoulders, the same head sagging between the two men and the way it looked on the pavement outside, Moxie with blood coming out of his mouth, Gloria and Peerless Percy on the bed, the sycamore tree in the moonlight, Justin—on the rock, in the water, sitting opposite me in the kitchen, the feel of his skin under my hand, the way he looked in my dream. The pictures of him were like a rope pulling me up there. I don't think I actually thought going up there would solve anything—what was there to solve? But it's as far as my imagination went.

Mickey came thundering down when I went through the gate and gave a couple of loud barks, but as soon as he smelled me he loped over and licked my face.

The door was unlocked. I didn't turn on the light. Moonlight filtered into the hall from the dining room on the right. I went upstairs and into Justin's room. There were no curtains, or at least they were drawn back. I could see his bed quite easily. He was asleep.

"Justin," I said. And then more loudly, "Justin."

I was going over to the bed when he moved and sat up. "Who is it?"

"It's me. Charles."

He switched on the light beside his bed and then sat up. "Charles! What's the matter?" His shoulders looked brown against the white pillow.

It all spilled out like a lanced boil. "Moxie's dead. That creep Percy kicked him downstairs. He and Gloria were. . . ." All the words for it had gone out of my mind, which was funny, because nobody I knew was backward about using them. "They were on my bed. . . . It's my fault. Moxie had made a big mess on Gloria's bed. I guess that's why they were on mine. I should have stopped him going all over the house. But everybody was away. Gloria left me this—" I pulled the news clipping out of my pocket. "You know why I don't have a father? Because he's a drunk. He died on skid row. He just walked out and left me. Him and his putrid medals. He walked out on me. I always thought it was Mother's fault. That's why I wanted—" I saw Justin reach for his robe and pull it around him as he got up. "Easy, Charles. Easy."

But it was too late for that. The gasps seemed to come up from my knees, shuddering through my body. Justin reached me and put his arms around me and held me while I cried out of some ocean I didn't know was there. I couldn't stop. After a while he lifted me up and carried me to the bed and lay down beside me, holding me.

I could feel his heart pounding, and then I realized it was mine. I couldn't stop shaking; in fact, I started to tremble violently. It was like everything—the water, the sun, the hours, the play, the work, the whole summer—came together. The golden cocoon had broken open and was spilling in a shower of gold.

Even so, I didn't know what was happening to me until it had happened.

When I woke up I was alone and in the bed rather than on it, which was the way I had gone to sleep.

The sun was streaming in the window. My pants, sweater, and jacket were over a chair. I had on my shorts. The first thing I remembered was Moxie. Then I remembered about my father. Then I remembered coming here, and what happened after.

I lay in bed a long time thinking about it, and the more I thought about it the worse I felt about myself, about Justin. And yet . . . somewhere, for a long time, I had known—not that this would happen, but that something would happen, and then everything would be over.

After another long while Justin came in. I didn't want to look at him.

He put a glass of orange juice on the table beside the bed. "Good morning."

I didn't say anything. He went to the window, stared out for a bit and then turned around, leaning against it, his arms crossed.

"Do you want to talk about it now or later?"

I sat up and drank some juice.

"Are you worried? About yourself?"

Right on. But I still didn't say anything. I wanted to be left alone. I wanted somehow not to have to think about it or talk about it.

"I don't want to talk about it, Justin. Let's just leave it."

"I don't think that would be a good idea. For you. Your first impulse is to run. So you'll run from this and then spend unnecessary years worrying about it. There's nothing about it to worry you. You reacted to a lot of strain—and shock—in a normal fashion. At your age, anything could trigger it."

"You mean it doesn't have anything to do with you?"

"It has something to do with me, sure. But nothing of any lasting significance. It could have been anyone—boy or girl. It could have been when you were asleep. You must know that."

Yes, I knew that. And I knew all about the male and female in everybody, too. But I was remembering other things. The times, lying on the rock, two of them, that I reached over and touched him. I had touched him. Not the other way around. It scared me so badly I couldn't think of anything else.

"You're snowing me. I don't believe you."

"I'm not snowing you. I know what I'm talking about."

"I bet you do."

There is nothing in that morning's conversation that I am not bitterly ashamed of. But of all the things I said I am most ashamed of that and what I said next.

"What does it make you?"

"I've known what I was for a long time."

And so had I. Without knowing I knew it, I had known. What did that make me? I stared at him. "Then why did you—"

"Did I what, Charles?"

That was what I couldn't bear. He hadn't done anything. I'd done it all. Always I had reached across to him. And the more I thought the more I remembered the times he had stopped me. What had I been going to do? I knew, I could tell, I was hurting him. But I was also frantically doing something else, something I do very well: I was turning it all off.

"I don't want to talk about it," I said again.

I'll never really know whether or not that was, in its own strange way, a last appeal to him, a plea for help before I blew up the last bridge between us. But I know now that Justin had reached his limit. He couldn't help me any more.

"All right, Charles. Have it your way. I'll be downstairs if you want me."

Justin had said, *The only thing you can't be free from is the consequence of what you do.* I was trying

not to think about that while I loitered over shower-
ing and dressing. But the evidence of at least one
act—giving Moxie the freedom of the house—was
staring at me. More evidence materialized around
noon with Barry. I had just gone downstairs. Justin
was working at his desk. I was trying to think of something to say. At least I'm glad about that. I was trying. Then I heard a car door slam and looked out
the window.

"Barry's here," I said.

"I've been expecting him."

I hardly had time to absorb that when Barry walked
into the room. Justin stood up.

"Hello, Barry."

"Hello, Justin."

They shook hands. Justin said, "You've come for
Charles."

"Yes. We had a predictably hysterical call last night
from Gloria. Apparently she had managed to talk her
father into letting her come back a couple of days
ahead of time because, she assured us, she knew he
wanted to get back to California. My own view is he
paid her to leave early. Anyway, I think she was
eager to get her version of last night's debacle in
first. She said Charles would be here, having wrenched
something out of her boyfriend who had got it out of
his kid brother."

"With counteraccusations, I take it."

"Of course. Nothing that could trouble a mother's
heart was omitted. I knew it was a mistake to have
our phone repaired."

The two men exchanged looks.

Barry turned to me. "I'm sorry about Moxie."

I didn't say anything.

"Think you can pass that exam? There's a letter
from the school telling you to report there two days
from now."

"He can pass," Justin said.

"Okay, son. Let's go."

I turned to Justin. "Good-by," I said. Then I added, "Thanks."

Justin was looking tired and strained. But he smiled. "Good-by, Charles. *Vaya con Dios.*"

"What does that mean?" I asked Barry as we got in the car.

He started the engine. Mickey, sitting on his haunches on the grass, gave a halfhearted "Whuff!"

We started to roll down the path.

Barry said, "It means, 'Go with God.'"

CHAPTER 12

I TOOK THE REPEAT EXAM at St. Matthew's and passed, and was back for the beginning of the school term ten days later. Mother and Barry, it turned out, had been married while they were apartment hunting. The period between the exam and the beginning of term was taken up with buying clothes and Mother worrying about moving into the new apartment. I had been braced for a lot of questions I didn't want to answer from Mother, and for the usual man-to-man garbage that both previous stepfathers had tried on. But no one said anything about anything.

I didn't think about Justin then or later at school. I was very busy and we were kept hopping. Sometimes, when we hit something in class that he and I had talked about, I could feel him pressing at the edge of my mind. But I quickly switched to something else. It was no sweat at all for about two months.

Then one day sometime in November, I was sitting in class, looking out the window at the gray sky and the brown branches of the trees. Quite suddenly I stopped seeing them. The sky was bright blue and the gold of the sun was coming around the green leaves across the window and I could hear the sea below. I could smell the charred wood in the fireplace, Mickey's dogginess sprawled in front, the tangy salt from outside. I heard Justin's voice and saw his face. . . .

I came to as I heard the teacher yelling at me in exasperation.

That night I dreamed about Justin. It was like the dream I had had before. But Barry was in it this time. He was holding the little snapshot of my father and saying, "But, Chuck, *he's* the man without a face. Not Justin." I looked at the picture and it was true. There was no face there. There never had been. I had just thought there was.

When I woke up I knew I had to see Justin. I had to tell him I was sorry for behaving like such a jerk that last morning. I had to make him believe how much I liked him. The word I had always disliked swam to the front of my mind: how much I loved him. I wasn't afraid of saying it any more, just sick with shame for—again—having run away. And I had to find Justin immediately to tell him all this.

After morning classes, before lunch, I left. There'd be no more roll call till that night. I walked out the gate without anybody seeing me. When I got to the main road I hitched a ride to the nearest town.

Late that afternoon, after several more hitched rides and a long walk I got to Justin's house. I began to be afraid Justin wouldn't be there when Mickey didn't rush out. The house was locked. I went to the barn, which was also locked. I came back to the house, found a window that wasn't locked, and got in.

There wasn't a lot of light left as I went from room to room. I knew now that Justin wasn't there, hadn't been there for a long time. It's hard to say how I knew this. The furniture was the same. His bed still had sheets and blankets on it. But the house had an emptiness that had nothing to do with furniture. It was terribly cold. There were some oil lamps around and I lit those when it got dark because the electricity had been turned off. I found some cans of soup in the kitchen, put some wood in the big range, made a fire, and heated the soup. Then I drank it with some crackers I found in a tin container.

I can't describe how awful I felt, worse than I had ever felt in my life before, like all the cold in the world was inside me. And I couldn't blame anybody. I think that was one of the things that was making me feel so sick. The other was the knowledge that was coming to me out of every wall and corner of the room: that the things I had come to say I would now never say—at least not to Justin.

After I had eaten I took down my favorite Terence Blake book to read. When I opened it a piece of paper fell out. I picked it up and unfolded it. It was a letter from Justin.

Dear Charles:
I feel quite sure that sooner or later you will open this book, so I'm putting this note here.

Knowing you, I am reasonably certain that you'll have a delayed reaction about that last morning that will cause you a lot of pain and remorse. Don't let it. You gave me something I hadn't ever again expected to have: companionship, friendship, love—yours and mine. I know you don't care for that word. But try to learn not to be afraid of it.

One other request: try to forgive your father. He did his best. More people do than you realize. A good way to start is by forgiving yourself.

My love to you always.
Justin

P.S. Barry is a good fellow and was a staunch friend to me when I needed one. Try to be his friend, because he's very willing to be yours. By the way, did you know he was an Army pilot during World War II? He doesn't talk much about it, but he might if you asked him.

I slept that night in Justin's bed, piling on every blanket I could find out of the hall chest. The next day was as cold and gray as I felt. There was wood stacked by the fireplace in the living room and I made a fire. Then I had some breakfast of more soup and crackers plus a can of spaghetti.

That afternoon I walked up the bumpy road to the cliff and looked over the edge to the flat rock below. Despite the two sweaters of Justin's I had found and put on, I was half frozen. Snow had not yet come, but it would almost any minute. The sea was black. The rock just looked like a rock.

That night I read through the book, had some more soup and a can of mixed vegetables, and opened another box of crackers.

The next morning I was shaken awake by Barry. He looked tired and unshaven and irritated.

"Between you and shotgun Gloria," he said testily as I rolled over and sat up, "my legal practice—to say nothing of my marriage—is not getting my un-divided attention. I suppose I should be grateful that Meg's only problem—for the moment—is food."

"Justin?" I said, although I was quite sure I already knew the answer.

"He died, son, about a month ago, in Scotland."

"Why didn't you tell me?"

"I wanted to wait until you asked."

"I behaved like a creep to him."

"Yes. But he understood."

There was something I was terribly afraid of. But I was going to ask it now, not a year from now. "Did he . . . How did he die?"

"He had a heart attack. Not entirely unexpected. He'd had some trouble that way." Barry stood look-ing down at me. "Do you mind if we finish this conversation downstairs in the kitchen? I started some coffee going. Besides, I don't have all those blankets."

"You will be relieved to hear," he said over the kitchen table, "that Gloria and Percy were married. The first, I can't help feeling sure, of what will be a series of marriages for her."

Dimly I realized that Barry was making conversation more or less to help me over this patch. I was trying to get used to his being there, sitting across from me, instead of Justin. I knew I never would, entirely.

"How's Mother? I asked finally.

"Fine. She'll be even finer when she knows you're back at school. Now that Gloria's married the two of you may have an easier time."

Barry stared into his coffee cup. "I'm taking you back to school, Chuck. God knows, you went through enough to get there."

The pain in me flared a little. I thought: And so did Justin.

"The point is," Barry plodded on doggedly, "are you going to stay?" He cleared his throat. "All opinion to the contrary, I'm not completely dim-witted. Evans isn't either. He said you could come back this time. But not again. I'm not your father. It's no use pretending I have any authority over you. And you've spent most of your life fighting your mother. So realistically, whether you stay or not is up to you. You're free to do as you want. But you're going to have to choose."

So I had got what I wanted: I was free.

Barry got up, washed the coffee pot and his cup and left the room.

You can be free from everything but the consequences of what you do.

A wave of misery washed back over me. But after a while it went away.

Barry appeared in the door. "Well? Where shall it be?"

"School," I said.

As we passed the living room I stopped. "Justin's books, the ones he wrote. I'd like to have them."

Barry was at the front door picking through a handful of keys. "Okay. Take them. They're yours."

I was staring at the keys. "How did you get in?" I hadn't thought about that.

"With this." Barry held up a key.

"How did you get it?"

"It came to me as executor of Justin's estate." Barry looked at me. "The books are yours, Charles. All of them. And this house. Justin left everything to you."

I couldn't think of anything to say, so I went in and collected the books I wanted to take with me.

As we left I said, "What happened to Richard and Mickey?"

"Before Justin went abroad he gave them to a guy in Vermont who seems to have his particular talent."

"You mean he's a writer?"

"No. His other talent, for salvaging flawed and fallen creatures. Himself included."

And me, I thought, as we drove through the gate.

ABOUT THE AUTHOR

ISABELLE HOLLAND was born in Basel, Switzerland, where her father was American consul. Later the family lived in Guatemala and then, for twelve years, in England where she attended private school, boarding school, and Liverpool University. In 1940, because of the war, she and her mother went to stay with an uncle in New Orleans where she completed college at Tulane University with a B.A. in English.

Miss Holland went to live in New York in 1944 and worked for LIFE, MCCALL'S, as well as in other branches of publishing. She lives in New York City, and is the author of two other books, *Cecily* and *Amanda's Choice*.